THE TIDE

by

Amelie Roane

New Platonist Collective
Publishing

ISBN 978-1-8381496-0-4
A CIP catalogue record for this book is available from the British Library

Introduction

Welcome to the Adjustment Programme. We have found that some preparation increases the chances of success. Please familiarise yourself with the following documents as you wait for treatment:

1. Enid's Diary
2. Barry's Letters
3. A week in the life of Amy Wu
4. Pascal's Investigation
5. Space Sickness Part 1

After you have completed the five documents please proceed to the final section entitled Afterword.

ENID TOXEQUO'S DIARY
Or
A natural history of the Leviathan of the Stars

August 14, 1984

They say its a terrible thing to kill a spacewhale an act of barbarism which will mark the soul forever. All I can say is them people never once met one, never looking deep into its ragingeyes and felt the deathwish deathlonging there.

The spacewhales range the galaxy in wheeling arcs along the ancient paths through the stars past nebular plumes and the orbits of pulsars and comets. They are older than the earth born from the death of the first stars and filled with Octavin the energy source which can light up entire worlds the most precious treasure. This Octavin is what we seek what we hunt what we live for and the leaking threads of spacewhale bloods what pays the price. They are elegant brutes.

But im gettin ahead of myself.

Im the sort of girl that has a chest full of VHS tapes a shelf of scifi novels a bustup old bike and an et poster. We had moved agin this time to UK Rendlesham Forest base. Pap is in the air force. Trueblue not pissy english. Im fifteen or thereabouts. Whenever i can i get down to readin and watchin scifi. Homework familytime schoolstuff aint nothin. Scifi is my life. Of it all theres none so good a tale as of the Cetasta. The spacewhale of the Hoshihenro show. From sunrise to sunset and dusk til dawn this is my existence the spaceships quarrels battles challenges wounds tech loveaffairs agonies and all suchlike.

Cant remember when it started when i decided to make a spaceranger of myself and go off in quest of adventures. Got myself my craft *Rosin* by clockin out me ole bike. Made my spacesuit printing up some grey sweatshirts. And my spacelance from this old telescope.

I am marooned on this desolate moon. I left my home long ago
zooming into space. But now what remains of humanity is in great
need. They are running out of life and falterin. The spacewhales
contain worlds of life. My quest is set to search out these beautiful
dangerous children of the stars. That death might be the portal to
life.

Tue September 2
First day of the new school and rode in on my bike Rosin. Didnt
want to come here but had no choice. Pap made the choice.

Crunchy gravel underfoot in the courtyard red brick buildins tellin
me onna stone its been there over 400 years. Puffed up punk faced
pigs. Pap sendin me to this wagamuffy multidough school with this
starchy scratchy uniform. They all think theyre better than me. But i
will show them. I will prove that im just as good as them. That i
can be better.

But i dont want to be here. I don't know anyone and somehow
every step and word is a gouge. It smells funny here like a death
hospital. There is something lumpy in my throat and my eyes are so
hot.

They gave me this locker for my things and I couldn't even open it.
I stood there and I knew i would be late for class because I couldnt
get my pencil case and timetable and map. The lock had this code
on and maybe i forgot the code maybe i couldnt work the lock
properly or maybe i was just shaking too much to be able.

These kids are sharks and they smell blood in the water.
Spacesharks i mean. The strong devour the weak in this dumpster
reality.
    -     Hey yankiedoodle let me help you.
He undid the locker for me.
    -     You want this?

A group in my class had taken my timetable. I tried to grab it but they threw it between each other.
It went on too long until they ripped it apart and spread the pages around. I got on hands and knees tryin to pick up the torn pages.

Just fooling around they said as they spat on me.

Went to the teacher like they all say to do.
He called us both in.
- We were just playing a game. We didnt know she couldnt take a bit of fun.
- Very well. Be a little more thoughtful please Devins. Enid we will look at how we can build your resilience.

Thing is, after commin home after all that I am more psyched than ever to get myself a RAD device. That's the way to go into Hoshi-Henro. Leave behind this sad world. Its like some tech to boost you up like some path to the stars of summit. Gotta get meself one of those. They say some dude is gonna bring one to the next convention. Have. To. Go.

Wed sep 3
In school was waitin for some snacks inna line at break time with all the little freaky coins pokin my hand. Then that boy came with his friends.
- What you getting he asked.
- Dunno maybe some chips.
- No chips here. You mean crisps.
- I know what i want.
- Cos if you want chips you should go to some burger joint. Hey sure you dont want a burger.
- Dont want a burger.
- Probably cos you already had one for your breakfast you yanks love those burgers so much.
- No aint had no burger for breakfast.

Oh he said and leaned in close to my face.

- Check out the whiff on this. She stinks of
  burgerbreath.

Burgerbreath burgerbreath they all chanted again and again. For the
rest of the day thats all they called me and even other folks started
callin me it. I dunno maybe they forgot my name or summink.

As i left school on Rosin they shouted it out at me and tried push
me off. I need to start bringing in some serious kit.

At home I plunged into my scifi trunk to shut out this world spikin
me all over. It was like those replicants. If you are not one of the
crew then you are one of THEM.

Thurs September 4
At school.

They lined the corridor all stickin out their legs an trippin me up as
i tried to get to the library. At the end before the double doors
stood Devins with his hockey stick. I would not run away or back
down. I was ready.

- Hey Burgerbreath.
- Whatchew want?
- Do you play hockey
- Hockey is on ice and theres no ice here so what you
  even yappin about.
- We do not play hockey on ice. Seems like you need a
  lesson. Lucky I am here to teach you how we use a
  hockey stick in England.

He waved it around my ankles as if about to hit.

- You better be careful with that there mouth o yours, I
  said.

-     Oooh what you going to do.
The stick hit my knee. It was only hard enough to sting a little.
-     I must inform you that not only am I an American
      citizen but the Captain of a whalin vessel, spacejumpin
      and fully armed with Octavin torpedos and
      spacelances.
-     You are seriously weird.
-     You have been warned.
-     Look burgerbreath whatever Raygun does over here
      youre not the boss of us. You gotta pay your
      subservience. Get it? We are going to smash you up.
He whacked my legs so that I fell to my knees. He prepared to hit
again.

I took my taser out and tased him. He screamed and fell down and
wet himself.
-     What the - you have weapons?
-     I warned you. Taser standard issue. Issued to all
      crewmembers.
-     Its not allowed i will-
-     What you gonna tell?
He quietly crawled off.

Fri Sept 5
Next day news had gotten around. Not sure if folks were afrighted
or didnt like americans or what. Cos they stood their distance.
Suited me that way.

Turned out the work were way harder than what i thought. It
would be no easy thing to show them what i was made of so hid
away in that school library every day. Workin and sketchin o
spacewhales.

Mon Sept 8

Every day on the way to that school took my craft, peddlin away. Got to thinkin wonderin what that school really is. Cos fine and super dandy its a school but i know that but i aint no schoolkid but a spaceranger and i dont ride no bike but have a spacecraft and my mission is to hunt a spacewhale an get enuf octavin for our dyin worlds. So question is what is that school. I figured could be some penal colony planet or some spacestation of the tiumi bloodsuckers or ole blackbeard pirate base. Only way to find outs to be careful an make sures them ones dont lull me into any false securities. Like S2E7 where they thought they had a friendly ship SOS but then them pirates took over an was a battle to win agin.

Tue Sept 9

- Hey newgirl. Hey.
- Don't you bother gettin toe know me. Won't be here long. Jus dockin for a year or two say then be flyin out agin.
- No hey, you dropped your er...was going to say radio antenna but its more like a retractable cattle prod...well not entirely sure what it is.
- It is a spacelance.
- Its just well I suppose its none of my business but I thought it looked a bit dangerous.

He turned to leave an that would have bin the end but there was somethin about him that I couldnt quite work out like maybe he werent one of these empty holograms all around jus workin off central AI programin like there was some spark in him of life or somethin like i already knew him an met him but had somehow forgot him like long ago in a distant land like the smell of sun still on your skin when the clouds have come. So I shouted out.

- Whatchew call yurself?
- Barry.
- You seem like an adventurin sort of fellow.
- I don't know about that.
- You ever seen Hoshi-Henro?

- Oh no. My parents they...I'm not allowed. You see they know that there are those er nudie scenes.
- The Japanese and French seasons of the show sure are wild but its the seasons 4 and 5 that Im into its all trueblue American style, huntin them spacewhales. You should come over and watch with me.

He came over to the shed with the beanbags and posters and stacks of candy and we slumped down in. … we watched S4E8 more. It did have some nudie bits.

- Whatchew think, i asked.
- It was ok.
- I am on a mission to return to my ship the hoshihenro you see.
- Right.
- Just gotta find myself one of these RAD things.
- What is a rad?
- Reality Alteration Device. That will get me back. There's a rumour passin through that one of these things is passin around the fan circuit.
- So we are going to look for it.
- Suppose so. But first we gotta kit you out boy. You ain't even got any spacecraft let alone any spacelance.
- Im sorry why do i need those things.
- For our mission. We continue the video in our lives. We are hunters. We cannot forget our true identity.
- Im not sure about all this.

Silence rolled over us like the wash. I needed to persuade him to grab hold of who he really was who he could be if he opened his mind and remembered the pulsing stars and the elegant curves of our engines. I would have to lead him along give some carrot. Somethin that might motivate a fourteen year old boy to do some crazy as hell stupid stuff.

- I reckoned that mayhap you mighta been HURO in disguise.
- Who row?

- No HURO you jus saw him onna screen.
- Was he the one with the er…
- Abs. Yeah. Im basically in love with him.
- I look nothing like him.
- Yeah pretty good disguise huh.
- But
- Cos if you were him then Id have to take this off. We are tight we are.
- Are you saying what I think you are saying?
- Do I have to spell it out.
- Yes.
- I'll let you see my boobs if you are worthy enough.
- Ok so lets say I am this HURO.
- Maybees you are. Im not sure. Thing is HUROs plenty brave and you seem like some scaredy cat.
- I can prove im brave.
- Yeah?
- Kit me out.

He took the spare cycle in the garage once we found the puncture.

Later Mam asked me what was goin on.
- Who is that boy?
- Thats Barry from school.
- A friend thats great petal.
- He is kinda a friend but also a followers cos im the captain and he is a subordinate crew member. Im basically his boss.
- Its nice you found some folks to share that tv show with.
- Also hes hanging around cos if hes brave enough he might get some sugarkisses.
- Oh a boyfriend.
- Not a boyfriend. I dont really want a boyfriend. Dont think he really wants a girlfriend. He just wants to see somethin for real. I want a brave crewmember. I suppose you could say its workin for us we jus want it all for real not a dream.

- Friendship is a wonderful thing my dear. Though your pap dont know nuffin about it tearing us up and away every few years for that motherhuffin dream o bein a commodore. Somedays i dont think he ever had a friend in the world cept me. Dont turn out like that precious. Try your best to have a friend.

Fri Sept 12
At lunchtimes i hid inna school library. Most days skipped lunch so i wouldnt have to see all them ass faced kids.

Today Barry sat next to me as we tried to do homework.
- Why do you do all your homework here isnt it meant to be done at home it is home work.
- If i do it now then when i leave at the end of the day i dont have to think about this place again until tomorrow.
- Right. But whats that under your books.
- This. This is some distraction the Hoshihenro encyclopaedia.
- So thats a thing.
- Sure is. And if we are gonna make a spaceranger of you then you will need to study it. Here have a look.

He flicked through. He was bein plenty careful with the pages an I hoped he wouldnt see how worn and used the character profile on Huro was.
- They say theres some secret message inside. But never mind that i need to show you the fauna of the galaxy. To know what to look out for.
- Ok.
- I will try not to do an exposition dump on you. Me i love it but im thinkin youre in it for the story not the worldbuildin.
- Whatever you think best.
- Ok so basically earth destroyed through environmental summink and the remainder of humanity is in spaceships lookin for a new home. Headline that the only thing keepin

us going is the energy source Octavin. Which is only found in livin space creatures. But thing is that you can't fire missiles or stuff at them because then they would explode and you would lose all the Octavin. So you gotta hunt them with spacelances - get em space creatures all killed but not kab-lewey.

- Space monsters.
- Dont look like that. Theres spacesquid and space-eels and moony cudcows. But they aint jus space versions of earth creatures. That would just be silly.
- Yes silly of course.
- They arent made of carbon based life form filled with water and respirin. They got there whole own fink going on with i dunno silica based life or something like that. We just call em all those earthy names cos they look a bit like em.
- Ok so to power all the spaceships and keep civilisation going we have to find this Octavin in these life forms.
- Yes. And chief of these creatures is the Cetasta.

I made a reverent pause for such things are beyond our ability to speak of and who can truly describe the sight of one of these creatures because we dont see them just in our eyes but in our hearts as if they was the very bones of the universe keeping it up in their long windin paths.

- The spacewhale. The largest creature in the cosmos. And all filled with Octavin. But they aint easy to find and even if you do how you gonna slay such a mighty beast.
- But getting a spacewhale would give enough Octavin to find a new home planet.
- Yes and we would be heroes.
- So your dream is a dream of death. Of killing and black blood and the joy of battle.
- Yep.
- I find that hard to relate to.
- Im not saying im gonna kill a spacewhale. Might be me that ends up slain.
- Im not sure thats any better.

-    Let me show you the galaxy at least.
-    Yes i think i can do that.

Sat Sept 13
Me and Barry had a day of adventurin through the galaxy in search of Octavin. Or a RAD.

Wheelin our bikes our spacecraft through gullies of pines. Evergreen forest never droppin for the fall ever-livin seemin endless indomitable but all planted to be killed by the forestry commission in long corridors of unmade cabinets and shelves and books. Like the Forests of Kudor from S2E4.

Trees of horse chestnut with branches drooping from despair the first drops of their hard shiny tears all giftbright in the fall light. Reminded me of summink but cant say what now. Beatin through nettlepaths taller than our heads the jungles of sound-jellyfishes in the Heptin Nebula. Tired out fields of stubble to scratch an claw our fleshy ankles like the replicants risin with their claws from Planet 56. Redblue stripples of berry stained pants showin jus like the haze of blood of moonfaced gasbuilt lil cudcows of planet Arognard. Messed up ole pigpool. The ochre worms of swirlin debris from banged up old supernovae like a stew of gnawed bones of the universe all mixed in and swirled up all soupy like. Cars streakin down lanes. Noodle eyed old robots in flash dogships sweeping round through rock battered ice sheen of freeze planets and the thaw of thermobeams on em extractin the h2o. Asteroid fuzz in the distance the endless waves pounding and grasping an trying to hold onto the land but some things you cant hold em close no matter how tight you try.

Dead planet after dead planet. No life on em. Never will be. No home for us. Always movin on pilgrims through the stars on our path o desperate survival an longin for summit green an growim an some wind on our cheeks once agin. Some openin. Somethin made for life. Some distraction from the depths of space which could be lookin at infinity for all we know the brain not made to see such draggin depth will suffocate yer mind if you look too long too deep. Leave you with nothin left infinity sucked yer brains out.

Finally tired and back in my wide yard after a day of adventurin.

Sunset all warmy an the air all clear an smellin kinda sweet with the yellowed honey of old ancient light. Sittin on the ground could feel twigs and gravel and grasshapes all pressin into my legs an Barry shiftin around tryin to get comfy an wishin for some plump plushy cush to sit his hiney. Tryin to light some campfire there fore it got dark with the sticks from trees. Theyre too green he said but they werent green they was brown with these lichens on them. He told me not to but I gone and got some gas from the shed and thrashed it all over. Lit it up but then it got smokey smoke an our eyes stung with the blue swirls and we coughed and had to move away.

Had to pinch some cutted wood from the outhouse gathered in my arms and threw it an then the flames came all whooshy.

Got coupla bags marshmellows an we got some sticks and spiked them up and then as the cold waves o dusk spilt round we toasted ourselves up. Mellows gooed up and cracked and turned all toffee brown onna outside our own innards too somethin warmed.
-	So Enid he said what planet have we landed on.
-	Not been mapped innit. We is probably first spacerangers
	ever been this far out of the shippin lanes. Virgin territory.
Barry started snortin like a pig. Think it was laughin. Whats so funny.
-	Its just its just
but he had lost control
-	Vir vir vig
but he was gigglin and rollin and alternatin cryin and fartin he were laughin so much.
-	What youre laughing cos i said virgin.
And then he laughed like a great barking dog and I joined in cos he was laughin so much and he looked so crazyass mental.

Later it got proper dark and we sat in blankets with some cocoa from the hut and tried to tell the scariest story. He wasnt very good at it but i told the story of ole jackie macknee from tennessee. Its too long to write here. He were well scared think he wanted to hold my hand but he were even more scared of that.

The stars spread overhead like crazy bright eyes of a million bats far away and I could even see the vulva of the milky way up there always promising something i could never tell what. I could look at them stars forever and try to figure out what theyre trying to say. We settled into mountains of blankets with the warm glowlogs between us.

In the morning it was dewdamp an fresh and i put worms in his hair. Spaceworms.

Tue sept 16
It was breaktime at school and was showin Barry what could be found.

- There sleeping the great beast itself. A spacesquid.
- Are you sure because it looks an awful lot like it might be the headteacher's maserati.
- Spacesquid no doubt about it. See the tapering head the luminous eyes the telltale yellow armour epidermis.
- But we arent after spacesquid but the whales.
- All is fair in love and war.
- What does that mean.
- Dunno pap always ses it. But thing is we need all that Octavin we can get. Sure its just a teaspoonful compared to spacewhale but still can power a craft for months. Adrift in the great dark abyss of starlight we betta take what we come across.
- Now you mention it, it does look a lot like those pictures of spacesquid you showed me if you squint your eyes.

He squinted his eyes an looked all earnest like and eager to please.

- Exactly. So we gonna charge it.
- With your er spacelance?
- Yes.
- And do I have to charge it too?
- Maybe if it were a spacewhale but a squiddy only needs one hunter. You get ready to grab the carcase.
- I will stand just over here.
- Yes thats right.

I took some steps back to my craft brandished my spacelance and started my run fast as i could. The beast almost threw me from my craft so hard was the impact.

But I wounded it the silica glass smashin and the shards splashed around. A pool of black blood spread underneath. Dismountin I attacked the mortally injured squid slashing at it with my lance and subjecting it to my wrath. For great was the storm of my wrath and it blew strong a hurricane of devastation. And it was only after much destruction that my anger was spent.

A crowd had gathered by this point to watch the killin. Strangest thin they didnt thank me for my deed but jus stood a-gaping. Then a teacher invited me inside no doubt for a formal thankyou and a certificate of commendation

His name was quinn or somethin. He said he were a social worker but to me he looked like he had that vampiric sheen in his eyes markin him out as one of the Tiumi bloodsuckers. Best be careful.

- Its not youre in trouble he said.
- Thats swell.
- No its more than that. Criminal damage. However. Your parents are being called in we are hoping to deal with this in an informal manner. Rather than pressing charges.

- ...

- Miss Toxequo I just don't understand why you did this. I know that this has been a difficult transition for you. That

you have not made a good start to this school. But why the
headteacher's car?
-    You wanna know the truth?
-    Of course.
-    It isnt a car its a spacesquid and I am captain Enid and i
     am a spacewhale hunter on the Hoshihenro.
-    This is another concern. This pretend play has gone too far
     and is veering into delusion. What might have been a
     harmless escape mechanism is turning into...I dont know
     what.
-    I dont mock your beliefs.
-    Your parents should be here soon. But i am afraid that too
     many red flags have been raised i am going to have to send
     you in for some assessments. It may be that this space
     mania is a variant of a recognised condition.
-    Yeah I will do whatever tests you want.
-    Ah here are your parents.

When we got back Mum and Dad clawed their way through my
stuff and found the chest of wonders.
-    Ill get a fire goin outside and we can put these on.
-    Its harsh honey but itll help. We cant have you saying all
     these things about thatem show to the authorities. No no
     no.
-    Cut it off at the root.
-    Lets go through, what is this crud. The Empire Strikes
     Back?
-    Oh no hon keep that, I like that one.
-    Isnt that part of this space nonsense?
-    No her show is that Japanese one the Hoshiwotsit. This is
     by some americans george lucus. Its kinda fine.
-    What about these books. Shouldnt reading be safe.
-    Far from safe. Jus look at what shes got there. Choose
     Your Own Adventure. That cant be helping that overactive
     imagination.
-    What about these books Philip K Dick. I dont want my
     daughter reading books by a dick.

- Hes fine. That stuff aint too much about space. Though kinda hard to imagine actually wish theyd make a film of it all.
- It just came out at cinema i said but they didnt hear or want to hear.
- Lets dig down here: Star Trek, Battlestar Galactica, Doctor Who.
- Take them off to the bonfire dear. They cant be helpin.
- And this ET.
- That one made me cry its alright. Its by the guy who did jaws.
- Planet of the Apes. Forbidden Planet. Tron. 2001 a space odyssey.
- Chuck them all.
- Ulysses 31
- That one sure is bad pretty close to the rot.
- Look here we are. Hoshi-Henro seasons 1 to 5 on videotape and assorted books and notes and character sketches and schematics.
- Thats what has to go for sure. Hun like any medicine it aint pleasant but we have to do it. Seein that smashed up car...

I didnt say anyfink i knew there was no point when they were in a mood like this when they had made up their minds and agreed about something. Best thing was to try an rescue some stuff while they werent lookin.

Fri Sept 19
They took me to this special assessment room and there were bundles of papers to fill in and a man who was tryin his best to look kind but who just seemed tired.

They were kinda fun the tests.

I got a flyer about the next Hoshihenro convention in Hoshi-newsletter. Its comin up soon. They say one of the stalls will have a RAD device. I gotta go.

Saturday sept 20

Leaning on the ridge with our binoculars. Me and Barry. The farm with its barns below us.

I had scouted out this base before an knew we could pull off some crazyass cool heist.

Lookin through the binoculars Farmgirl had gotten out of the tractor and goin to meet her boyfriend by the barn door. They got busy with their lips an then she led him in by the hand. Now was our chance.

- You see that there space hauler i said.
- That. It looks awfully like a farm tractor.
- Thats where youre wrong mister.
- Ive got a bad feeling about this.
- No we arent doing star wars.
- What.
- Never mind. We must commandeer the hauler as space rangers. It should be good for the hunt.
- You want us to take it. Steal it.
- Its not stealing cos of our authority.
- Do you even know how to drive a tractor.
- Hauler.
- Ok hauler.
- Covered it in basic flight. You gotta get yourself on that course man.
- I havent seen it advertised.
- Got one on jupiter base comin up.
- Yeah so…
- So we are gonna take it.

-      Maybe i will just er watch. You can leave me the
        binoculars. I can be the lookout.
He were clutching them eyeglasses so his finger went white and it
looked like he was going to really freak out now.
-      Are you part of my crew or not.
-      I guess.
-      The captain has given you an order. Should you not obey
        then you will have to be put off the crew.
-      What you mean.
-      This aint gonna work if you dont join in.
-      So if i want to still er...see your er...
-      I will not be removin any part of my uniform for a scaredy
        cat.
-      Right.
-      So you comin.
-      I suppose so.

We ran out like smeakcats and i jumped onna tractor and pulled up
Barry after. Startin it up we trundled out of the farm and onna lane.
-      We are doing it said Barry.
-      He was happy and i even gave him a go steering.

We drove down lane past fallin leaves all brassy and it was easy real
easy to drive the thing this way and that and it felt so fast though it
couldnt have been so fast cos its just some small spacechew. This
lane then a bigger road then all kinds a criss crossy canterin roads.

Out onna a12 with a big queue of cars behind and then a policecar
bluelights wailing stuck behind the traffics.

Policeman was kinda grouchy when we was caught. He didnt take
out no cuffs but got us all shamefaced.
-      Didnt realise it would be so much trouble i said. I dont
        want to get into trouble.
Barry all staring at me for tellin big lies and he looked like his eyes
were gonna cry.

-   I will drive you to your parents said policey. You will have
    to explain yourselves to them.

Tuesday 29 September
Showed Barry the leaflet for HoshiCon today.
The Third HoshiHenro Congress
Fan Conference
Connaught Hall, London
                7   October

-   I am gonna go. Wanna join?
-   Is that a school day.
-   Only a Friday.
-   I don't know.
-   They say that there's gonna be a RAD there.
-   Remind me what one of those is again?
-   Reality Alteration Device. It's how I'm gonna get back to
    my ship the Hoshihenro.
-   Are you sure that's...real.
-   If its not I'm really sunk cos I never heard of any other way
    back to the stars. I'm not sayin there isn't another way jus
    that I never heard of it.
-   It might just be er gossip and rumours.
-   Yeah it might still be in Detroit and the fan magazines
    sayin it will come to London are still all wrong.
-   That wasn't quite what I-
-   So, you coming?
-   I don't want to play truant.
-   I can get the tickets and we can go onna train.
-   But I dont want to miss school and get into trouble.
-   You wont get into trouble Ive got it all worked out. The
    perfect cover.
-   I just am not into it as much as you.
-   Do you not understand how much I want that RAD to get
    out of here.
-   Even if i did believe it...I dont want to lose you.

-    You dont have to lose me. You can come to the stars too.
     What do you have holding you here after all?
-    I dont know the trees and the fields and the waves. They
     won't have those things in space.
-    If I cant appeal to your devotion to the cause let me appeal
     to your sense of duty.
-    Duty?
-    Yes. Do you still want to see these.
I made the gesture.
-    Er yes.
-    Then youll have to come.

Mon Sept 22

It was that quinn agin. This great fat fake. Yes thats right he were a
lil porker. Rolls of it under his chin lookin like pale grubs set out in
rows. Been busy suckin blood i think.
-    They arent sure what you have, he said.
-    Whatchew mean?
-    You did all those tests and assessments right.
-    Yeh.
-    You were meant to come out with a diagnosis. Dissociative
     disorder. Paranoid delusions. Schizophrenia. Something.
     But you came out clean.
-    But im not mad. I jus see reality differently. To me Hoshi-
     Henro is the real world and this is the pretend one and
     why should I be blamed for makin this world a little more
     real.
-    But that isnt how anyone else sees it. They think that you
     are deluded. Dangerously so. So much that they think you
     have some sort of condition.
-    But why cant they just allow me to be myself without
     slapping these labels and conditions on me.
-    Its the way the world works. People cant just believe
     anything they like. It has to correspond to something.
-    Thats dumb.

-   So Enid what will it be?

-   ...

-   As you think about your answer there is another issue
    which i have to raise with you. That is your joyriding on a
    agricultural vehicle. By all accounts you should have a
    lengthy criminal record by now. It is only through the
    leniency of the authorities that you have escaped. No
    doubt they wish to gently nudge you in the right direction.

-   ...

-   But i think you need a sharper jolt to come back to reality.
    So i will tell you some home truths. i know your type. I
    know that you are rotten to the core. That you will never
    amount to anything. That everything you touch will turn to
    shit. That you are a useless lazy stupid failure and socially
    retarded and that you have ruined your own life before its
    even started by just essentially in your own nature being a
    screw up. Its not even worth wasting the time on you. It
    would be better for the world if you did not exist.

-   I will never give you the keycode to the mainframe.

-   What.

-   This interrogation or whatever this is. I know what youre
    driving at but no amount of abuse will make me betray my
    crew. I will not give you the keycode.

-   Just shut up he said sighing.

Next

It was the day of the trip to London for the convention and getting
my hands on the RAD. Who knows maybe it was hearsay that the
thing was there. But I had to try. I had to get back.

I had faked a letter sayin I was off school for some extra freak
assessment. I got my tickets already. So arrived at Sutton train
station early inna morning all ready and nervous an excited. But as I
stood onna platform I saw a group enter the station. It was the
deputy headteacher and two police and Barry half hiding behind a
girder. It was a right ole trap.

- Betrayer, I shouted at Barry

He pretended not to hear but was blushing.

- I am going. I am going on the train.
- No you are not, said the teacher.
- You're coming with us, said the police.
- I won't I won't I won't.

They had to drag me kicking and screaming and dissolving into crying and clawing. But soon the train arrived and then left without me and I fell onto the floor weeping and wailing. My chance had gone. I would never get home.

Can't remember much of the rest of that day between police and school and parents. They were all angry. But I was angrier by far. At Barry.

- I was just trying to do the right thing, he said. You've got to understand.
- I don't want to talk to you again.

Sat

He was knocking on the door a long time before I let him in.

Barry been tryin to apologise but as far as I am seeing finks he is all locked up inna brig. He no crewmember no more.

- I don't know what to do to say sorry, says he.
- There's nothing you can do, I said. You lost me the chance of getting myself a RAD. That was my chance to leave this sorry world behind and get back where Im meant to be, in the stars.
- Isnt there any other way?
- Mayhaps there is. If I can get enough Octavin then I'll be able to power on to the ship, spacejump up there, and bring enough for us to rebuild our dyin civilisation.
- Ok, let's do that then.

I decided that just like HURO I would have to give him the chance of redemption. But he would have to earn my trust again.

- Only way to do that is to slay a spacewhale.

- Isn't that what we've been trying to do this whole time anyway? I don't think that…I mean how is going to be any different now?
- Cos I just saw a spacewhale path. Come on, this is how you prove you aren't a betrayer.

We got ready. All togged out and sat on our craft. We will hunt a spacewhale. We flew along the paths with dust flying up at the crunch of our tyres. Past fields and hedges and finally down a thing I think is called an escarpment, and stood onna top of the ridge looking downward. I stood in bold outline, hair breezing behind me in the crazy wind. Barry cowered.

- There it is, I said. Spacewhale path.
- Are you sure that's a spacewhale path? Because it looks an awful lot like a train track to me.
- To them uninitiated there sure is a certain similarity to the patterns. Though of course them spacewhale paths are made of quantum fluctuations rather than sleepers and rails.
- And you're going to?
- Jump onna top of it and slay it wiv a lance through the top of its skull.
- And that isnt dangerous?
- Ive been telling you from the beginning that this stuff is dangerous. Its real you know.
- I…I don't think that this is right Enid. I think that you are trying to jump onto a train.
- If thats what you think then clear off. I have no business being a crewmember wiv anyone who cant see the way things truly are. I have my mission. Im not gonna let you screw things up again. I gotta get back to Hoshi-Henro.
- Look what do you want me to do?
- When I say jump then jump.

The spacewhale came around the corner all huffin and puffin with billows of plasma leakin out of its freak spout. I had my lance ready and Barry gripped my hand too tight and as it passed below us we jumped together. I had planned on slayin it there but we couldnt. On its roofy head we were thrown back by the whistling air ripping into us. There we had to grip on as tight as we could or we would have been flung down to the ground, all the while as the smoke from its spout left us coughing and desperate.

It musta been almost an hour we clagged on until the beast made its stop in Dunwich by the sea. Shaking and gasping we was then in no shape to fight and kill a spacewhale so we slip off and staggered away. But still rode on the back of a spacewhale best roaring coldknuckle of me life.

Sitting on shingle shore bag of vinegar fries hot. Warmin ourselves jus as we need.
- I think its time to call it in. Retire. We did well, said Barry.
- You did well. We mighta not caught it but what a ride. Today I saw that shadow of HURO in you.
- What?
- Today you didnt just fly on a spacewhale. You flew above your cowardice. You died to it. And I am readmitting you are a crewmember.
- Great. Thanks.
We continued eating. It was getting late now and we would not be able to make it back home tonight.
- My aunt lives here in Dunwich she will let us stay over if we want.
- Thats a fine thing.

We continued sitting as the sky darkened and moved from ragged grey to black tarry pitch and the wind which had snatched at us day raised its voice and tore at us. The roiled waves and the whorled wind stirred up a wildness within us and we spun and ran and jumped. In the dark too dark the edges of the waves were all foamed in weddingwhite from the moonlight and out there somewhere in the sea were the low moans of spacewhales circling the globe with their mournful song like they had lost summink though god knows what. Shingle underfoot tossed us at weird angles til we slopped around skatin on these millions of tiny wave nibbled rocks from ice ages past. Most of the time barry were a shadow not a person as we whipped close to the ice waves as they swung in and then we ran back with sog filled trainers. And then the wind built up mighty strong like a iron claw punchin us about and we crashed into each other and i could feel his breath was warm on my cheek then we flew apart as if we were part of that wind and screamed into it screamed our souls into it because with its howling no one else could hear and that was just as we wanted it. And finally the storm swallowed us up in its flat drops something like pain something like relief. For now everything was fine. Maybe it wasnt all so bad after all stayin around here.

Monday 1 Nov

Pap call us in.
- I have some good news to tell you, he said
- Whats that, I asked.
- I just got ourselves back to the US. Been promoted to Commodore. We'll be shipping out to Atlanta next month.
- What.
- Yes we can thank our lucky stars. I finally caught a break.

I did not know what to say and stood there like a dumb mute. Inside it was like a storm rising. Finally I spoke
- I don't want to leave.
- What do you mean?
- I don't want us to move again. I want to stay here. I was just starting to get used to it here and get to know people and I was making real progress with my hoshihenro things.
- We don't always get to choose these things hun.
- But you chose. You chose to be Commodore. You didn't have to you could have stayed here.

- Now, said Mam. Lets all take a deep breath and a step
  back. What we've got is good news but it's hard news as
  well and we need to get used to the idea of it thats all
  because its a mighty shock outta nowhere when we didn't
  even know you was thinkin about it.
- Now there's some months to get used to the idea just
  wanted the two of you to be the first to know. How about
  we get a celebration meal on the go?
- I'm not hungry, I said.
- You better start showing some gratitude girl. I come here
  with the best news our family ever had and you throw it in
  my face. You gotta shape up.
- Hun she's only young.
- Not that young, he said. Now, what you say. Will you join
  us?

I roared and ran off to my shack in the garden.
- Give her time, said Mam.

Later
Was raining an I could hear the dripy drips on that wavy iron of the
top roof inna hut. Been in a whole day now.

Barry came in and I was in the corner smushed in on the floor
hiding my head on my knees. Pretended hadnt seen him.
- Whats wrong Enid? You havent been at school and
  nobody will say why.
- Theres no point going there now. In a few weeks we are
  shippin out.
- What?
- Paps gonna be an assistant Commodore in Kentucky.
- Back to your trueblue then.
- I aint been there for ten years i was five when we left dont
  even know what a trueblue is. Thing is it all stinks. Jus
  when we was gettin close to slayin that spacewhale an now
  have to start from the beginning at a whole new base.

Train up a new crew why i dont know if we have that much time before we all run out of Octavin what with the sonic jump and all.

-    Itll be alright.
-    You cant know that. We might crash into a black hole onna way.
-    Enid.
-    So yous havin to cash in your reward for all this time.
-    Enid youre crying. A lot.
-    So you can see them. What youve been wanting all this time.

So I reached to lift up my top.

-    I dont want to see them.
-    What am i just so ugly now i disgust you?
-    No its not that i mean i do want to see your er well its just not like this with you crying and miserable and well it isnt what i wanted. It wasnt meant to be a payment i thought maybe you wanted me to see and didnt at the same time and in the end you could persuade yourself you wanted me to see more than not. It was meant to i dont know. But i dont want it now. Not like this.
-    But if im unhappy for the next few weeks and then go you might never get it.
-    I can live with that.
-    Then everything you did was just because you wanted to do it.
-    I didnt want to do it all im a wuss remember. But it was fun because it was with you.
-    Its almost like having a friend.
-    Almost.
-    Just dont forget im your superior officer.

Still Later

Barry left. Pap came in.

-    You got to stop this sulk, he said. We is shippin out and thats that.

- But we just got started now.
- Then theres not too much to root up. Cheer up hun were finally gonna get the dream. Commodore thats some pretty hot meat.
- But my dream aint to be a commodore its to be a spacewhale hunter.
- But thats made up love.
- How come your dream of being a commodore is real where mine of bein a spacewhale hunter aint?
- I tolerated this while you were little but you are growing up and need to grow out of this. Yew gotta...don't yew understand yew gotta live inna real world. In a few short years you will be pulled into adult life. You gotta enter real life...tarmac, bosses, abattoirs, budgets, factories, weapons, arguments, weddings, profit margins, engines, schools, prisons, contracts, newspapers, hospital wards, warehouses, correspondence, pipes, rape, money...and above all the relentless quest for mastery; in the family, in the office, the parliament, the canoeing club. Mastery over others, and ourselves. Pre-eminence.
- I don't want to.
- George no. That was Mam when she saw his face.

He grabbed my arms tightly and looked deep into my eyes all angrylike.

- There is no Hoshi-Henro. No spacewhales. No Octavin. No HURO. Nothing. There is nothing at all to believe in.

I felt all faint and it all went black.

They told me there were sirens.

In the hospital.
Barry visited me inna hospital.

- They say i have a rare heart condition. Normally fine but now it has been inflamed by stress. In a sticky situation.

- What do they say?
- They want me to give up all my sci-fi. Says that it has led me into distress. They found out about jumping on that train too. They think I tried to kill myself because of the depression or something.
- Oh Enid.
- Pap was right though. I see that now. It was all stupid. They've made me realise. It is just a TV show. I've been pretending. I've just immersed myself in fantasy to run away from difficulties in my life. They say I tried to escape the concrete, the interactional, the emotional elements of life. So I became consumed by the works of my own imagination. I just wanted hope that life could be different. Hope for a life that is not empty and friendless and depressed.
- No.
- What do you mean?
- It is real.
- You dont actually believe that though do you. You were jus playing along.
- Maybe at the start yes. But then something gradually happened. I started believing. After all who gets to decide if it is a bashed up maserati or a spacesquid? Why should they get to decide. Who gets to decide what is real and what is fantasy? Why can't so called 'real life' be part of a bigger story that itself. Like maybe there could be this great story that covers everything and everyone and which is bigger and than our little lives. Like there could be a way of seeing that makes sense of it all and combines it into one whole rather than dead facts. That maybe, somehow, we could all be in this story too but that the story took us over and swept us along in its arcs, like an invisible tide.
- Can such a story exist?
- It would have to be as wide as the cosmos and as long as eternity and be about brokenness and death and indestructible love. It would have to have the most epic battle scene ever between good and evil. It would need to

be about how humans are so complex and messed up but leave us somehow with some hope. And it would need a hero. A hero that could shake the cosmos. And the story should be everything and come and take possession of us.
- Sounds kinda crazy.
- Maybe it's like a dream. Dreams seem very real when we're having them. They seem entirely self-contained: you wouldn't think in a dream that you need to wake up and join the real world. But maybe there is a greater wakefulness, a deeper reality than this one that we are in now. A reality that corresponds to this one but which entirely transcends it. Who can claim such a thing does not exist? It would be like a dreaming man claiming that there is no such thing as the waking world.
- Ok i see your point.
- We trust the evidence of our eyes and thats good. But sometimes our way of interpreting the world can stop our eyes from seeing whats really there. Back then, before, you carried my faith, even though i didnt myself believe all this stuff. Maybe now you can lean on mine.
- Thankyou Barry.
- Now lets get that heart of yours better. We got a hunt to go on.

A week later
I was glad when they let me out of that stinking boxhouse of death and back into the open air. The smell of the hunt was in the air.

When I met Barry morning came very dim. Distant and faint. The mists crept around the valleys and the little pockets of trees and hauling our bikes we found the spacewhale tracks again. Or as Barry said
- It still looks a little like a railway line.
We looked down in silence for a few moments thinking about what was about to happen. Finally Barry spoke

- Looking at it now I am having second thoughts. After all it
  didnt even work last time. What is different this time?
- Our courage failed us. Now we are resolute. What is
  needed is a head on contest not jumping on its back. Only
  by staring down the whale will we be able to slay it.
- We?
- Auxiliary Barry you must be ready to harvest the corpse.
- Oh yes. Definitely. The corpse. What about you?
- I will stand in the spacewhale track and halt it with my
  lance.
- A er spacewhale is many many times your mass.
- Yes over 1000 times.
- You will get squashed.
- But this is how it works.

He hesitated for a moment as if torn in two directions at once. This
what he said.

- It might look a bit like a train line but im convinced that it
  is a spacewhale trail.

Got onto track. Could see spacewhale comin along. Had myself a
powerstance, lance aloft. That beast shone in the morning light the
massive tonnage falling towards like a draining dream. Then the
screeching noise the most terrible screeching cuttin up my
eardrums. The thing with its ragingeyes and flappingtale and then
was when I saw that deathwish in the eyes the pressure of Octavin
from inside the weariness of bein so old older than mountains tired
of the life of it longin for a resty sleep. That great hurtlin heavy
friendly death flew toward me and my lance. I could see every detail
of its face as it slowed to gobble me up. Thought for a moment
maybe it were a train and i would be slayed.

And then the craziest of all slowin to a stop on the touch of my
lance.

The whale lay immobile before me. I whooped and cheered. I had
done it. The spacewhale had been slain.

THE LETTERS OF BARRY HINCLIFFE

Cromwell College
Dunwich, DW1 3EF
06/10/89

Dear Enid,
You will have to use this address in future when you write because
term has started. I have now started university.

Earlier today my parents helped me to bring all my belongings
on the train and there was a great rush or porters and cabs as we
were directed to Cromwell College, and then a mess of students
and parents as everyone tilted at getting themselves sorted out at
the same time. My parents, the two of them, sat themselves on the
edge of my narrow bed; actually my Mum perched on the edge of
the bed and my Dad leaned back but with no part of his body every
being still or coming to rest. I tried to spit out some words but I
wanted them gone. I didn't want the other students on the corridor
to see my Dad's fungal fingernail or hear my Mum's shrill fake
laugh. So I told them it was time to go and we had an awkward hug
and they left and then I rearranged my things from the way they
put them and sat down at the desk and it was suddenly very quiet
and I wasn't quite sure what I was meant to do. Then I
remembered that I could write to you about my new life. And that
is what I'm doing now.

There's a week of activities to acclimatise ourselves to the city
and university but I just want the course to begin. You and I, on
our separate paths, have our different methods but we are aiming at
the same thing: The Reality Alteration Device. You are going off on
a madcap adventure hunt to track down this thing (thanks for the
postcards), which is of course entirely consistent with everything
you have done before. Whereas I will study hard at this physics
degree and crack the science behind Reality Alteration and
construct the device. We'll see which out of the two of us achieves
the goal first. But that's why I can't wait for it to begin properly -
because that's why I'm here, our great dream of making it to the
stars.

I have read from the great wad of paperwork they gave us that there is a Hoshi-Henro society at the College. Of course I will go along but I don't know what to expect. They can hardly have the same perspective on it as the two of us. I suppose that if I go along I might get to know people here, but at the moment i don't feel great about that: it's all so unfamiliar and strange and now I'm here I don't know if I made the right choice at all. But at least I know that I have a greater purpose in being here.

Wish you were here,
Barry

***

Cromwell College,
Dunwich, DW1 3EF
11/10/89

Dear Enid,
You wouldn't have had a chance to receive and reply to my last letter but I thought that I'd write anyway as it feels like so much time has passed already.

I have never met so many people in my life as I have come into contact with in the last few days. There has been an induction into the physics department; tours of the city itself; college talks about fire safety and study skills and registration with a doctor; tutor group orientation; the matriculation ceremony; the inaugural College Dinner; flu inoculations; and so much more and all the while the milling and spreading of students.

Perhaps chief of these things was the start of term disco in College, or rather it was probably more of a shindig (I am reliably informed) as it was live music rather than what we are used to. Not that I am used to it at all, even from school. Now, do give me some credit, I did actually go to this disco. I walked in and saw lots of people drinking and dancing and standing in groups. As I didn't know anybody and didn't know what to do I walked straight out again after doing a circuit of thirty seconds. I took refuge in the Upper Levels of the College, still able to hear the beat of drums in the deep. But here's the thing: I wasn't the only one hiding away up

there from the gyrating orgy below. There were others. One of
them Faiza, had built a Faraday cage to enclose her portable radio
in preparation for arrival; so we put that on and we wired for some
pizzas (yes you can do that here!) and at some point someone got
out a board game which we stayed up playing into the morning. So
all in all a fairly decent start of term party. I wonder what you
would have done if you would have been here? Something so crazy
that I couldn't even imagine it, no doubt. I hope you're staying safe
out there in the wilds of the USA and that you don't do anything
too dangerous.

Take care
Barry

***

Cromwell College
Dunwich, DW1 3EF
16/10/89

Dear Enid,
We have now had the first of everything - first lecture, first tutorial,
first lab session, first assignment and first meeting of the College
Hoshi-Henro Society.

But before I tell you about them all - thank you for your letters.
So you have heard rumours of a RAD in New Orleans, kept under
wraps and passed around in the swamps? I don't understand why
such secrecy is really necessary - why can't they just say what it is
and leave it in a public place for everyone to use, if it really is
genuine? But I suppose it's the same reason that I don't tell people
what I'm doing here - we'll get shut away in an asylum or mental
health ward or whatever they're called these days. Your travels
seem to be going well but I don't understand how you can afford
to go off travelling like this. It's not like you're rich and your
parents don't exactly approve of your Hoshi-Henro interests. But
now for some of those firsts I was talking about:

First Lecture - We started with some Newtonian
mechanics, fairly similar to the stuff which we covered in school

(ok, I did it at school, I can't even guess what you picked up). It was therefore familiar and a bit boring but despite those things came at an incredible pace. By the end of the lecture I wondered when we were going to get to the exciting material, the cutting edge stuff about quantum interactions and astrophysics and dimensions: all the things I will need to know for my task. As the lecture closed I got the impression of time rolling out like a scroll forwards for many years before we would be able to get beyond these basic teachings into the science that I need. I realised then that it is going to be a long and difficult path to gain the knowledge that I need to make a RAD. Thinking now, I don't know what I imagined, that I would stroll up and after a few weeks would casually put together what has proved beyond the abilities of our best minds? But despite all this I am resolved more than ever to press on and devote myself to this task.

First Hoshi-Henro Society meeting - I don't know what I expected but what I found was a great variety of people with different levels of interest in Hoshi-Henro and who found various aspects of the show which attracted them. At this point it is not clear if any of them have a similar perspective on Hoshi-Henro as the two of us, but it is wonderful to be able to come to a place and unite with others over something that you have in common. For the first time here in Dunwich I felt at ease, almost at home. Obviously we can't actually watch any episodes here in the environs of Dunwich, but there are some other activities that we can do - a read through of an episode and a discussion based on the back of this, plus a singalong to the theme tune and the music of the closing credits - the President, or Prez, of the group, Josh, has a guitar and leads this with great gusto and I was quite moved when the first chords twanged out. After the meeting finished and we left the room I hung around in the corridors with a couple of others from the society. I can't remember what we talked about - this and that, the show, the college - but it was quite nice.

That's enough for now. Soon these things will not be firsts but part of the continuing routine of my new life, hard as it is to believe that now.

Stand by for action!
Barry

***

Cromwell College,
Dunwich, DW1 3EF
24/10/89

Dear Enid,
I'm sorry that the report from New Orleans turned out to be a
hoax. I hope that you manage to get more reliable news in the
future as your search for this enigmatic RAD.

Here in Dunwich things are starting to settle down from those
dizzying first weeks of whirling impressions. The worst thing is still
collecting my dinner from the servery and casting my eye around to
see if there is anyone I know that I can sit next to, or settling to eat
entirely alone. So just like school, just when I wanted to get away
from anything that felt at all like school. Still, at least now there is
an expanded list of people that I can seat myself beside. There are
several people that I have even got to know fairly well. You might
even if you were brave start to call them my friends, if you didn't
know me better:

Faiza - she is very clever and studies maths. She likes very involved
board games and all things technical and above all mathematics.
But her willingness to talk is limited to subjects which hold her
interest, namely (1) circuitry (2) the history and peculiarities of
Dunwich (3) Prime Numbers up to 1000 (4) board games (5) brain
teasers. She talks a lot about these things. I am sure that she would
be a great asset in my quest for a RAD, but unfortunately she has
no interest in Hoshi-Henro at all, and given her personality, would
seem to show no interest or indeed possibility in extending her
range this far.

Matt - After the last (or should that be first and previous) meeting
of the Hoshi-Henro society, he was one of those that I hung about
with. Since then I have eaten breakfast with him etc. He is fairly
easy-going and fairly straightforward to talk to (esp. Compared to

39

how intense Faiza can be). He does however have an interest in beer that I do not share.

Elanor - I met her at the HH Soc too and was talking with her and Matt.

Amy - Unlike the other three who are part of Cromwell College in the first year, Amy is on my course and part of my departmental tutorial group and a member of St. Peter's College in the old town. She has given to sitting in the same sort of place as me in the lecture halls. Now, before I started here I somehow imagined that everyone who managed to get into Dunwich to study physics was, like me, a little bit of a geek. But Amy seems to have that sort of effortless cleverness that means she can achieve results and yet still be considered popular and cool and doesn't have that nerdiness that comes from isolation in the library and seclusion with equations and books. Anyway, it's really annoying and she keeps on trying to make jokes during the lectures to me when I'm trying to pay attention. She says she likes HH, but I regard her interest as ephemeral.

So these are a few of the characters that I have come into contact with. In a couple of weeks there will be a weekend away that the HH Soc is organising. I'm not sure whether to go or not. I know what you'd say - you'd make fun of my caution like usual - but what worse could there be than being stuck somewhere awful for a whole weekend, unable to escape, surrounded by people you can't bear.

Hope to hear from you soon,
Barry

***

Cromwell College
Dunwich, DW1 3EF
07/11/89

Dear Enid,
You certainly know how to write a letter to hold the reader's interest! The level of detail is incredible. Perhaps one day I will be

able to verify the truthfulness - or otherwise - of what you write. You might not remember this but in the UK we call it snogging.

Your own forthcomingness (is that a word?) makes me feel a bit guilty that I have not been entirely open with you. You see, the reason that I wrote so little about Elanor in my last letter was because I was not sure what to say. Or rather I was too embarrassed. But to put it plainly, I fancy her. There, you have it, I hope you're satisfied. Perhaps it was because of this that I decided to go on the weekend trip of the Hoshi-Henro Society. Which she also was going on.

We took the train on Friday afternoon and arrived when it was dark (I am afraid that I didn't pay attention to where the place actually was but it was pretty much the middle of nowhere). There must have been almost thirty of us as we walked from the station in the dark along muddy footpaths, torch lights here and the waving in our hands. After what seemed like a long time carrying our bags and luggage we arrived at the barns with our toes numb from the cold. There was a smell in the air of the growing things in the smoky cold of the night and also I want to say of something like a tired excitement and possibility and the wildness of it all as we tramped on together/ The barns themselves were simple - a room for the boys, a room for the girls, a kitchen and a meeting room. That last room was what interested us, why we had come, the chance to watch Hoshi-Henro for once, away from the radiation of Dunwich. After a hearty dinner of chilli con carne we watched the first episode of our glut, all packed in together, and the remainder of the night we sat around in groups chatting. I was mostly with Ellie and Matt wondering if I should splurge to them your and my suspicions about Hoshi-Henro, that it is all real. I didn't have the guts to open my mouth and say anything on that night. But I felt a sort of pressure growing within me.

There's something a little unnerving waking up in an unfamiliar place with unfamiliar people. Despite this, morning brought bacon baps and herding in to watch more Hoshi-Henro together. The afternoon was free for us to use as we wished with some playing an elaborate game in the fields, others going on a run, some strumming on guitars, a couple reading and so on. I mostly drifted around unable to settle to anything because inside me like some sort of burning thing was the need to say something to see if I was the only one who thought HH was real. And not knowing if I would step and say something, or not, was driving me crazy. I couldn't eat much that night and was twitchy all through the evening's episodes. I felt too hot and all itchy. Around 9pm we flowed out into the cold dark night and some of the leaders set off fireworks. Afterwards we sat around campfires with cocoa, toasting marshmallows. It must have been around midnight and Ellie and Matt were next to me by the fire, and looking deeply into the flickering flames and leaning close I said that there was something I wanted to tell them: 'You're going to think I'm crazy…' I began and then told them all about our own thoughts (you and I, Enid) and adventures and our plans for the future. When I had finished there was only the crackle and hiss of the fire.

'Sometimes I think that same thing,' said Ellie, 'but then I think that it can't be so if I'm the only one.'

'Me too,' said Matt. 'I sort of hover between the two, not quite sure any minute which is the case. But what you're saying…I feel that it's right.'

It was very tentative but by the time we stumbled back to our sleeping bags we had agreed between us: Hoshi-Henro is real and one way or the other we would find the path to the stars, our true home.

The next day I was tired but felt new and clean and exchanged significant glances with Ellie and Matt over toast at breakfast. After some more episodes in the morning we had some quick sandwiches for lunch, hefted our luggage and made the long walk back to the station. It had only been a couple of days but had felt much longer and somehow significant. I now definitely had friends and together we were united in a greater purpose - ad astra. It felt good. On the train back, sitting in front of Matt and Ellie and leaning back to talk to them I felt a little giddy - whether from sharing my secret or finding acceptance or tiredness or from being so close to Ellie (which was becoming intoxicating) I couldn't say.

I'm still a little high from it all, back in my little room in College, and need to sleep - goodbye Space Knight!

Barry

***

Cromwell College
Dunwich, DW1 3EF
16/11/89

Dear Enid,

I'm not sure you needed to send me the telegram. It wasn't urgent. Goodness knows what the messengers thought. Seriously, who sends a message: BUT IS SHE HOT? E. I will not dignify it with a reply, except to say that she is very beautiful, at least I think so, though I have heard others call her plain which I don't agree with. In any case she talks to me and smiles at me and seems to like being with me which is more than most other girls - even you, if you remember, mostly scowled at me or at least set your teeth into grim determination. I find myself trying to arrange my days so that I can catch a glimpse of her or have lunch with her.

Which brings me to an awkward circumstance. Because of the aforementioned desires I tried to set up a time together with her alone, one to one. I don't call it a date because I wasn't proposing anything else than friendship. I just wanted to spend time with her because she was becoming the light of my life. So we set a time and a day: Saturday, 10am, and I waited eagerly.

On Saturday morning I pressed the doorbell of her house precisely at 10am. There was no reply. I tried again. Eventually Ellie's head popped around the door with bleary eyes. 'Sorry,' she said. 'Can you give me half an hour?' I agreed and walked up and down the street in the cold many times before returning at 10.30am exactly. She let me in and made a cup of tea, apologising. She had only just woken up because on Friday night she had been out dancing with Matt. I tried not to let it show on my face that this entire idea was making me feel sick. But she went on to say that they had only been out together 'as friends.' Whilst I was sure that this is all that it was to Ellie, I was starting to get worried about Matt. After all, it seemed like he was interested in her, and they

have common interests and he has some sense of coolness about
him - he studied English. He may well have the edge on me.

It was still lovely to be with her though for that hour.
Nothing will probably happen between us though.

Stay safe,
Barry

***

Cromwell College
Dunwich, DW1 3EF
01/12/89

Dear Enid,

I can see how you are able to write that way but I assure you that
all thoughts of the RAD have <u>not</u> fallen out of my head to be
replaced with romantic notions. But still, what you say is crazytalk:
'why not simply tell her how you feel' - nothing could be worse
than this. By a single stroke I could lose a friend and co-conspirator
and these things are too precious to lose. But even worse than that
I would lose <u>her</u>. She would feel too awkward to be around me and
so I would no longer have the enjoyment of being with her, and be
starved of her presence. I know what you will say, that I don't
know how she will respond, but I can't presume anything else
based on my general experience of life so far (though this girl Amy,
the annoying one from my physics lectures, keeping on bugging me
to join her anti-Rhoades campaign, aiming to change the name of
the college for obvious reasons. I'm not interested - it's a new
experience to try to discourage a girl). I'm not exactly a popular guy
when it comes to the ladies. Even between the two of us, nothing
really ever clicked in that regard.

In that vein, I'm happy that you've found someone to travel
around with. I have at times been worried for you travelling alone
in the wilds of America and have at times imagined the worst. So
I'm glad it's worked out for you and that you have some
companionship on your epic road trip, as you called it.

Progress through the degree continues to be slow, though at
least now we are starting to cover some more interesting material:

lectures on Special Relativity. I am starting to see some prospects here - the idea of different frames of reference. Perhaps that is all the Hoshi-Henro world is, a different frame of reference. All we have to do is to align our own world with that other. Exciting if I can make it work. So you see, all this is bubbling away in my mind, even as I am thinking about Ellie.

Barry

***

Cromwell College
Dunwich, DW1 3EF
08/12/89

Dear Enid,
It is already the end of term here and the beginning of the Christmas holidays. So I have travelled back to my old home and you will have to write to me there. So much has happened in these months that I feel like an entirely new person. I knew that I believed in HH before but now somehow sharing this with a group of people has made me enter into it more fully. Now it isn't <u>your</u> crazy idea that I've tagged along with but my own that I'm living. Or maybe it's just nice to have some friends. It is really hard to pack up my things and leave for the break, Dunwich has come to feel like home in a way that my actual home never was. And of course it is hard not to be sad that I won't see Ellie until January.

Concerning Ellie, there is something distressing to relate. In our final Hoshi-Henro meeting of term, Josh the leader, leaned in to me and pointing to Ellie and Matt said 'You can see how much she likes him - you can see it in the way she looks at him.' I didn't say anything but internally was devastated. Is this where things are heading, that Ellie and Matt will be getting together? I hope not. I wouldn't know what to say.

But quite apart from that, I thought has struck me. Matt, Ellie and myself shouldn't keep our knowledge about the true nature of reality to ourselves. We should seek to let others know these incredible things. So my thoughts are this: Space Sickness Parts 1

45

and 2. You know, the episodes that were only ever shown in Japan
for contractual reasons. In those episodes it is reputed (though you
probably know more than me) that a space sickness breaks out
which causes the crew to start dreaming that they are on 20th
Century Earth and cannot escape and return to the ship. Well I
thought that we could put on these episodes as a way of showing
and convincing people of our ideas: obviously we can't film a sci-fi
show so we would put it on as a play. I'm trying to start on a script
based on the gleanings that I've heard of the original episode.
Apparently Matt has actually seen the episode whilst visiting Japan
so I will write to ask for his help to reconstruct it. But maybe he
will think that it is all a silly idea and that it would be no good to do
it. I don't know. I'll do it anyway.

Apart from that I'm looking forward to having a rest over
Christmas after an intense first term. What will you be doing for
Christmas? Will you be heading home to be with the family? I hope
that you manage to give yourself some rest and celebration - you
can't unceasingly and unstintingly be questing without tiring. You'll
need a break!

Happy Christmas,
Barry

***

12 Bredfield Road
Sutton, IP63 2AP
24/12/89

Dear Enid,
It is all coming together - Matt and I are working on the script for
the play Space Sickness. He only saw the scenes in Japan and
doesn't understand Japanese so we only have a vague idea of the
story, but we know the scenes and the action and so we will be able
to recreate it as best we can! Obviously there will have to be
concessions to the fact that it will be on stage rather than screen,
but I can hardly believe that we're actually doing it! We've also got
the go ahead from Josh, the leader of the Hoshi-Henro society at

College and so we will be able to recruit people from there to be in the show. When I first thought of this idea I thought it was too unlikely to actually happen and now it is going ahead I can hardly believe it - but more important the message about HH will go out so that more people can experience a taste of true reality, and that is the thing we truly are aiming for - to change hearts and minds.

A little ominously Matt said that he had met up with Ellie over the holidays (apparently they are only a town apart). He said that it was as friends but it sounds a little fishy to me. And why didn't I think to ask for her address - actually I did think but was too afraid to ask her because...I suppose because I was afraid she would see through the request right to what I really wanted which is her in all her fullness. I should just think of a really good reason to ask for her address - an unshakable excuse.

With Christmas wishes and best hopes for the '90s.

Barry

***

Cromwell College,
Dunwich, DW1 3EF
12/01/90

Dear Enid,
It is my first night back in Dunwich! Term starts tomorrow.

I was sorry to hear that your Christmas went so badly. I do think that you did the right thing in going back to stay with your parents - you had to give them the chance to treat you well rather than assuming that they wouldn't. It's such a shame that they are trying to treat you like a child. You are an adult now and you can make your own choices and if they can't accept that then perhaps you need to limit contact with them, just like you said. No more family Christmases. And I thought that Aunt Ethel was bad.

It is hard to explain what it feels like to return to Dunwich - the people and the place.

First the place. I didn't describe much of the city to you, partly because I know you've been here before but also because I was so caught u[in all the new things to pay too much attention to little details. But now I am returning and noticing: the walk through the bare winter marshes between the Old City and the Colleges on the hill, crossing all the innumerable channels of water, instantly escaping the chimney smokes and being in the fresh countryside. That's another thing about this place, the smog which often crowds the streets - thick fog and smoke combining. Then there's the wind which I think you'll remember, blowing straight over the North Sea and hitting the town and its streets and our faces like a slap. It is the coldest thing that I have ever experienced. Coming back to this place felt as if I was coming back to my place in the world, that I had found the hole that I fit into.

Next the people. I was very nervous returning because I had wondered whether that first term had been some kind of freak experience - that when I met my friends again everything we had would have evaporated, dried up by the empty expanse of the Christmas holidays. Or that I had somehow imagined that people wanted to be my friends. Or that whatever spark we previously had, it would be gone now. It was all enough to make me hesitate before knocking on Matt's door in College. But I entered in and sat on his bed and inhaled the scent of his washing powder and I smiled because suddenly I knew all was as it was meant to be and all was perfectly fine.

We had a lot of talk about now that we knew we would be putting on a production in a couple of months. I know it's a lot to ask, but do you think you'll be able to make it on 15 March? I know it's a long way, but if you just happen to be passing through Europe at that time then why not visit then…

I feel my description of Dunwich hasn't done it justice, so I include a clipping from a book on the history of Dunwich below:

The city of Dunwich, capital of East Anglia, was famously saved from the encroaching waves through the ingenuity of the ancient coastal defences before the great 1286 storm; a large chunk of the town of Aldeburgh to the south had fallen into the sea. The old city was shaped by its ten historic colleges. The oldest and richest is Greyfriars, set by itself amongst green pastures in a meander of the River Dunwich, it's tall spire pointing to the heavens. This most prestigious College is joined on the east bank by the River Colleges: Blackfriars, Temple College, the Victorians All Saints, St. Francis by the harbour, with its long lawns leading to the River. Around the headland stand the three seafront colleges; St. Katherine's College, St. Leonard College with its pier, St. Martin College; each with their own private beaches. The list is completed by the two big colleges at the centre of town around the marketplace; St. John's College, St. Peter's College; the chapel of St. Peter was known as the cathedral of the marshes and resembles a ship sailing out. Dominating the skyline of the old city is the Lighthouse Library, built upon the headland at the tip of the city and beside Hale's Bluff. This ancient structure has had continual additions through the centuries and its underground shelves spread over half the city.

Dunwich Institute of Education, which gathered up the singular colleges into one organisation in the 1880s, had only recently rebranded as Dunwich University; many of the old signs with the previous acronym were retained by stubborn academics or inconvenient architecture. Which was very confusing for new students confronted with what seemed an implacable instruction in the lobby of the physics building in ten foot high concrete built into a supporting wall.

Whilst tracing its history back to the middle ages, it was in the 1940s that its most distinctive element was introduced to the university. The Institute had won the bid for the Atomic Research Science Experiment; the UK's nuclear research project. Construction was quickly completed on the High Energy Physics Building – a great white gleaming geometric dome on the hill north of the city - and experimentation on a range of theories had begun, working in cooperation with the Manhattan Project in the USA. It was the research into electromagnetic pulses that the scientists in HEP B advanced most impressively, becoming world-wide experts. These pulses however had a drastic effect upon the city of

Dunwich. Whenever an experiment occurred, and the pulse went out, all electronic equipment that was not protected by a wire cage was damaged, often beyond repair.

Bereft of electricity, Dunwich became a city marooned in the past, an island linked to civilisation (if Saxmundham can be called civilisation) via steam train. No cars (spark plugs), no refrigerators, no computers or internet or telephones, no electric lighting, no radios or recorded music, no McDonalds. It became an idyll for luddites, anacrophiliacs, warm beer enthusiasts, and escapees from the patterns of modern life. And the tourists. Trainfuls of tourists. A slice of olde Englande served up, a must visit in all the guidebooks, a city wide theme park of Austen and Dickens and Sherlock Holmes. Buoyed by the large university and a never-ending rotation of tourists, the city was able to afford the street lighters, washerwomen, milkmaids, porters and stables that such an anachronistic situation demanded.

My college, Cecil Rhodes College, was created in the great expansion of the Institute in the 1960s. Work at HEP B was suspended for a year to allow for the building of new department buildings and five new colleges, and the new campus was based to the north of the river Dunwich. The resulting panorama of concrete and glass contrasted against the medieval streets to the south, and those submerged in nostalgia for an imagined past – incarnate in Dunwich city – were aghast, vilifying the Institute and Council for allowing such monstrosities. By the present day several of the buildings had been recognised as architectural gems of the 60s and were now Grade 1 listed. The brutalist Guthrum College, formed of great long slabs of concrete, designed by architect, Le Corbusier, was chief among these. Wuffingas College, a miniature of the Alexandra Road Estate, built by Neave Brown was not far behind. Fawcett College, with its womblike structure designed by Oscinda Lucido, was unique. Even Oliver Cromwell College, comprised of a fifty foot photorealistic erect phallus, was at least something to talk about. Cecil Rhodes College was not one of these noteworthy buildings. It was a squat structure with a peaked roof,

and could have functioned equally as a school, prison, hospital or
retirement home.

***

Cromwell College
Dunwich, DW1 3EF
23/01/90

Dear Enid,

The trail you've picked up in South America sounds both exciting
and very promising. To think there could be some ancient, almost
unknown, shamanic wisdom down there about a portal to another
world hidden in the leafy hot jungles. I hope you manage to stay
safe with all the rainforest trails and poisonous snakes and I will
send these letters to the Columbian hotel (is your 'friend' still going
to be travelling with you in the next leg of the trip?) I have to say
that the equatorial climate sounds welcome compared to the blasts
of icy winter whistling down the lanes of Dunwich!

Here at Cromwell College I have been recruiting the cast and
crew for the performance of our episode. But there has not been
enough people from the Society able to help so I have opened it up
wider. Amy from class - the annoying one from the lectures, too
cool and beautiful for a physics student - she is going to be in it as
Baleine. Even Faiza is going to help with something technical (only
she won't say what it is). But the upshot of all this is that there are a
lot of people to organise for rehearsals and it has been getting me
stressed out. I've been snapping at people and hardly eating. Ellie
must have been able to tell because one night she stopped at my
room and told me that we were going to sort it all out together and
organise everything. We sat down with pen and paper to sort
through and plan. However we did so - because it is a single
student room - sitting on my bed, our legs dangling off the side,
and I was beside myself. Here, a girl, sitting on my bed, and not any
girl but Ellie whom I cared about very much. We would only have
to lean back to be side by side in bed, only have to move slightly
and be in each others' arms. I could barely think and must have
seemed very nonsensical to her as I kept on edging towards doing

or saying something and then holding back from that great precipice. I think I ended up saying some weird stuff, flitting rapidly over topics and/or making some bizarre noises of frustration and repression. She probably thought that the stress of the production was getting to me. Although part of me thinks, and this might be wishful thinking, that she came to see me tonight, not to sort out lists and timelines but because a small part of her wanted to fall backwards with me as well. I don't know. Perhaps - though I don't see how she could be interested in me.

From Barry

***

Cromwell College,
Dunwich, DW1 3EF
02/02/90

Dear Enid,
I haven't heard from you but I'm guessing that you are deep in the Colombian jungle and in no position to sort through correspondence. Things continue much the same here. I study towards the grand mission of building a RAD. We continue to rehearse for the play which will show others the true nature of reality.

Only there is one incident I will pass on because of its awkward weirdness, I think you will appreciate it. Now and then Faiza helps me with my homework assignments. Not that we do the same course - but much of the mathematics is the same, and I find that she is very good at explaining the concepts. Anyway, we were working on a Condensed Matter problem and Faiza was cracking open the Ribena when I said it:
'I love Ellie.' Faiza didn't seem to know what to say and was going to gloss over it, so I added 'I'm in love with her.' Faiza took a swig of her joice: 'What is it that you love about her?' she asked.
'It's hard to say exactly. There are a lot of things that I like about her: her looks yes, her intellect, the way she treats others, our shared interests, her sense of humour, her nerdiness, the way she is

52

great to talk to, the way that she opens my mind to new things. The
way she smiles. She has a very wide smile. But what I love is simply
irreducibly her and the fact that when I'm with her the world
seems to be a glorious place and alive, set on fire with blazing light.'
'Ah,' Faiza said. She didn't say any more. I think I partly must have
chosen her to tell because I knew she wouldn't be interested
enough to pass on the information. Because that was the very thing
I did not want. But still, I wanted a little more back than an 'ah' or
else I could have told the four corners of my room.
'So what do you think?' I asked.
'It sounds like you like the way you feel when you are around her.'
'In a way.'
'Perhaps you like the feeling of being enraptured and not the actual
person?'
'No that's not it at all. I think you've misunderstood.'
'It is quite possible. It is very interesting, this human drive for
mating, but quite illogical, strictly speaking. For instance, you could
do an experiment with yourself correlating sexual stimulation and
your contact with Ellie.'
'I'm going to stop you there.'
'You cannot pretend that this is not a case of the sexual drive. You
must think of her in a sexual way in your mind to feel this urge
towards coupling.'
'I don't want to treat her in my mind as a sexual object for my
gratification, if that is what you are referring too. She is better than
that, higher than that.'
'I mean the act of-'
'No, we're not going to go there,' I said. 'Maybe we should go back
to talking about numbers.
'Very well,' said Faiza, 'only it must be very hard for you, seeing her
together with Matt.'
'She's not together with Matt!'
'Oh, I thought that they...'
'No!' I said.
'Not yet then,' said Faiza. 'You should get in first, you know.'

'Even if she would even consider me, which she won't, at the moment we have to concentrate on the show, this great mission of ours. This isn't the right time to start a relationship.'
'But you love her, or you say you do. I thought people say that this is the most important thing. If she really does mean that much to you then you should set all else aside and pursue her with all your might and main.'
'I have thought about it, believe me, a lot. But in the end there are things more important than my personal feelings and whether I have a girlfriend. I have to put truth and our mission to reclaim reality first.'
'Interesting, interesting,' said Faiza. 'I do find the human subject endlessly fascinating and educative.'

Watch out for snakes!
Barry

***

Cromwell College
Dunwich, DW1 3EF
14/02/90

Dear Enid,
A month to go until the performance now and we have been working on the costumes.

Today was some crazy party day at College - it was Founders Day. There is a great formal ceremony in the morning and then a grand lunch dinner with robes but then in the afternoon the real party begins with lots of bands playing and much quaffing of beer. I had a great load of it spilt over me and had to change my clothes. I didn't even feel like trying to join in after that. Fortunately Ellie invited me off site to her house to escape the madness. I think Matt must have been tied up with the festivities. At her place we made some popcorn and then went to her bedroom to escape the housemates coming and going.

Now I have never been in a girl's bedroom. Not even in yours when you lived in the UK. I don't know, but it felt as if I had extra

nerves coming out on my skin and that anything could happen and I was suddenly a whole lot more drunk of the charged atmosphere of the room than any of the guzzlers in College. After some time talking, she said:
'Oh, you can check my costume as you're here. See how well it fits.'
'Yes, good idea,' I said, a little weakly.
'Sit over there and don't turn around,' she said.

As I heard the rustle of clothes behind me those minutes seemed very long because I felt the pressure of wanting to turn around. But I didn't want to be the sort of person who would misuse her and sit gawping at her in her undies. After all, if I creeped her out and she thought I was perving at her then there would never be a chance of anything happening between us. But then, I really wanted to turn around and maybe it would be the spark that started something and soon we would be kissing. She didn't have to get changed behind me - maybe she wanted me to turn around and see her - or maybe part of her did. I willed to move my muscles but they were frozen - my body didn't want to aid and abet a peeping Tom. Whilst I was still thinking, she said: 'You can turn around now.' She looked amazing in it, just like she belonged to the world of Hoshi-Henro. 'It's a little short,' she said, flattening the hem against her leg. It really was too short for the stage but perfect for her room. 'We can have it adjusted,' I said. 'That's the advantage of doing these try ons well in advance.' Something lay in the air between us but I couldn't name it and I didn't know what to do. It was as if the whole world lay before me and all I had to do was reach out...so what do you think I did in this culminating moment? I believe you know. I did nothing.

It should have been the time to make my move, this perfect moment that everything was building towards. But I couldn't bring myself to do it *nor she me). Why? Perhaps because of the play. Perhaps because I feel unworthy of her because she is light itself. But above all, my mind is focussed on the performance. After that will be my opportunity. I will tell her how I feel.

I was relieved to hear of your safe return from the jungle trek. I don't think I would have tried the 'medicinal extracts' from the tribes. I don't know if you really will have any better luck further

south - but you have to try it if there's even the slightest rumour,
right?

Barry

***

Cromwell College
Dunwich, DW1 3EF
01/03/90

Dear Enid,
I don't know how to reply to your last letter. It was too graphic for
me, but unfortunately a compulsive read. Sex. There, I wrote it.
You've had sex. You're right (of course) that I've never experienced
anything like it or even remotely close to it before. No doubt you
think me a prude for talking like this. Or else jealous of your
experience. But the reality is that I have no use in knowing which
mechanical operations to perform or what to suck and when to
wait, and so on, as you wrote in great detail. I will most likely never
be close enough to anyone for such information to be of any use to
me. It is irrelevant.

Barry.

***

Cromwell College,
Dunwich, DW1 3EF
15/03/90

Dear Enid,
Today was the day of climax, the great performance of the lost
episode of Hoshi-Henro, and people came! There was an audience!
    First, the pure elation of the occasion - as the final scenes played
out and I heard from backstage I felt as if I were lifted in the air
and filled with ecstatic emotion. The message was going out and
what a wonderful message - of the true come that is awaiting us, of
a hope that lies beyond the stars and overshadows us, a deeper and

stronger reality than this brittle world. It was probably the best moment of my entire life, everything coming together like that. It was a high moment when everything seemed possible and the whole world expanded. Have you ever had a dream and in the dream you realised that you were dreaming and so you became indestructible no matter what is thrown at you? It was like that.

Second, in the celebration after the performance I was approached by Josh, the leader of our College Hoshi-Henro Society: 'Wow, just wow!' he said. 'I am blown away by that! And what I realise now is how selfish and fearful we have been in keeping Hoshi-Henro to ourselves. Do you realise that we are the only College in Dunwich which has a Hoshi-Henro society? That all of our fellow students have no opportunity to encounter the show for themselves? As I was watching I realised - we have to spread the message. We have to set up Societies in every college! And I'd love you to head it up.' On the other side of the hall, my eyes were drawn to Ellie. 'Thanks,' I said, 'I'll think about it.' And then I strode to the other side of the room. I wouldn't think about it, I would say no. Now was the time to concentrate on Ellie, not anything else, to tell her how I felt, and, who knows, perhaps be able to call her my own.

Third, I spoke to Ellie. 'I've got to tell you something,' I said. 'Me too,' she replied. 'Matt just asked me out and I said yes. We are together now.' For a moment I didn't know what to say. For it was Matt who had taken advantage of the mood of jubilation and asked her to be his. And when it had come down to it she had chosen him, not me. 'Congratulations,' I said, and hoped that it sounded less hollow to her than it did to me. 'That's really great for both of you.'

I hid in the toilets and quietly cried for a whole. Then I returned to Josh: 'I've thought about it, I'll do it. I'll take Hoshi-Henro across the university. 'Good,' he replied.

So there you have it. She is gone from me, and I have set myself on a course where I will not have time to be with her or Matt. It is probably better this way.

Barry

***

12 Bredfield Road
30/03/90

Dear Enid,

It is the Easter holidays and I am back at my parents again. I have started to get excited about the plans for our great unfurling - of new societies sprouting up around Dunwich, of our timetables and decisions.

I am sorry to hear that your South American expedition has turned out into such a bung. But at least you managed to gain a tag-along boyfriend. Do you think that they'll let him into the States? But where will you go next? Where will the wind blow you next in your search for the path to the stars. I sometimes imagine how you hear these rumours of strange and mysterious places - sitting around a campfire with the smell of canvas at the dead of night as bourbon is being poured, as the banjo strings still into silence, halting their vibrations, a bearded man in the shadows begins to mutter in a low voice; or perhaps your car pulls in at a gas station in the middle of endless cornfields, with the single attendant drawling and chewing, wearing a baseball cap, and then he sees your HH pin and he talks of another guy who passed through who mentioned a secret path; or a ramshackle store where some kid grabs your jacket and you bend down and he whispers in broken English of a place where the air feels different. Perhaps it isn't like any of these, but you must get the rumours somehow.

Hoshi-Henro seems more real to me than ever now, more than when you were here. I think back to the old times when we pretended those trains were spacewhales. We were playing really, even as we were trying to perceive the shape of the new reality in the outline of the old. But now it is like we aren't playing any more but coming to lay our hands on the substance of things - we are pressing on with great energy.

I told Faiza about our letters to each other. She says hello and asks whether the moist atmosphere of the jungles caused the spread of yeasty infections on your person.

Take care,
Barry
P.s. I am still a bit teary about Ellie.

***

Cromwell College,
Dunwich, DW1 3EF
03/05/90

Dear Enid,
Sorry that it has been over a month since the last letter but it has
been crazy here, spreading the news of Hoshi-Henro.

We started with a script reading and discussion at Wulfingas
College and we had to move to a larger room because people were
packed in too tightly. At Fawcett we began singing and never
wanted to stop. At Guthrum we moved quickly, putting on
interviews and life segments on the impact HH has had on their
lives. Rhodes College was a little quieter - we started a drop in cafe
where people could explore the show through artifacts and
reconstructions. Every night I am out at meetings at the colleges,
and afternoons are crammed with the organisation meetings for it
all. I would be tired from all the effort but the incredible uplift of it
is incredibly energising. People are coming and encountering
Hoshi-Henro and it is meaning something to them and they are
letting it enter and redefine their lives. It is as if, finally, reality is
breaking out amongst us. Every day the gatherings are growing
larger and every day we are going deeper into our great adventure.
It is hard to believe it is all really happening. And so far we are only
seeing to the hill colleges - the town colleges remain untouched and
a great clamour is arising for us to be involved down there as well.
We may need to get more people involved in our mission to help.

If all this isn't good enough in itself, there is another great
advantage, and that is, being so busy there has been no chance to
bump into or spend time with or even sometimes to think about
Ellie. I am trying to move on, you see, as nothing can happen there
any more. As Ellie is concentrating on her degree work (and Matt?)
she decided not to get involved in this HH expansion mission. It is

59

probably for the best. Hopefully, starved of any fuel, my fire for her will gradually grow low. Only in those last few moments between wakefulness and sleep, the times I am unoccupied, she rises in my consciousness, burning it. But this too will pass.

You still haven't said where you're heading to next. Enjoying the comforts and familiarities of North American life, no doubt, for now. Are you even going to attempt seeing your parents?

Barry

***

Cromwell College,
Dunwich, DW1 3EF
17/05/90

Dear Enid,

Hoshi-Henro has never before been this vital, this utterly real to me. It is as if I am already living in that other world, having a direct apprehension of the universe as it truly is; everything is suffused with the glow from that other world, bringing it alive, making it sing out. I find myself lost in rapture for hours, considering these great things and being carried away in glorious light. There are not enough words to tell of it all - the courage of the Captain, the strength of Huro, the intelligence of Eiko, the kindness of Itsuki, the brightness of Reiji, the truthfulness of Baleine, the cunning of Pequod. And the fearsome spacewhales, the hidden saviours. To enjoy and savour such things with my all - that is what life is about. That is what I want to spend my life doing until the day when at last all these things will become our very own and we will see face to face.

As you might be able to surmise, our great outpouring of excitement about HH continues to spread apace through the student sections of Dunwich. There are now societies meeting weekly in every college in the city, but more importantly more people are coming to know HH for themselves and find in it something of more value than anything in this reality. It is continually exciting, giving myself over to this work. Currently my major work is training up leaders because we are spread so thinly.

Yet still, exhilarating as it is, I worry that this great expansion is only operating at a surface level. That is, that these people are only coming to appreciate HH as a TV show rather than the vision of what undergirds all of reality and binds it all together. I long for people to have a true understanding of HH, as we intended from the beginning, for it to enter their very souls. Perhaps in all of the activity we need to draw back and to make sure that we don't extend ourselves too far and somehow miss what we were aiming at in the first place - to bring people into a new relation with the transcendent which pervades this world and constitutes true reality.

Love to hear your thoughts
B.
P.s. my end of year exams start tomorrow!

***

Cromwell College,
Dunwich, DW1 3EF
28/05/90

Dear Enid,
Events have turned sour here in Dunwich. It's the HH societies you see.

We have a little committee - all the leaders of the college societies, and myself and Matt. We were planning what to do next. I was outlining my hopes of running sessions to deepen our awareness of HH as constituting true reality - further leaders training, a 1-2- meetings network, and so on. And then whilst I spoke Matt cut across me to say that he wanted to lay out a plan. 'We have made good progress,' he said, 'in getting people interested in Hoshi-Henro. But our impact has been limited to students in a small town. What we need to do is to look outwards and create a movement that will ripple out through all of society. We need to upscale. Even recruit some staff. Key to all this, the need to monetise the current membership.'

I didn't know what to say as I heard all this, but what I did know was that I stood opposed to it all. It seemed as if Matt wanted to expand for the sake of expansion, an ever growing organism, trading off the popularity of HH to gain money. He wanted to change the search for ultimate reality into a fan club, where all people had to do was to like the show and not look any deeper. To make it a mass movement he wanted to let the true meaning of HH fade into the background and then quietly give it up. For Matt it turned out that it was all about numbers and money and influence within society. Success. But really I could see that Matt had stopped believing in HH. Now it was a vehicle for him.

I explained quickly to the group that this was not our purpose and aim and that we needed to re-form around our core mission. Matt in turn explained that a majority of the groups' members he had approached beforehand had agreed with him that his plan was the correct course of action.

As this news burst into the group the meeting dissolved into separate conversations amidst shouting and finger jabbing. For myself I stayed silent and numb. I had been blindsided. He had sewn it all up before I even had a chance to fight back or to salvage the situation. As the recriminations flowed, Josh at last stood on a chair and proposed that we defer all decision making for a week to give us all the chance to digest all the different plans and to understand them. The group gave their relieved consent to this idea and the meeting broke up.

With all this going on I'm glad that you're planning to come to Europe for your next trip - or adventure rather. I know that you say your main destination will be the Carpathian Mountains but maybe you can stop off in Dunwich on the way? Or at least London? It would be good to see you.

Sorry that your guy wouldn't come with you on your next trip. I don't know if you absolutely had to dump him because of it but I'm sure you know what you're doing. More than me in any case.

B.

***

Cromwell College

Dunwich, DW1 3EF

07/06/90

Dear Enid,

It has been a busy week. I had meetings every day with leaders in the HH societies - sometimes as much as four meetings in one day, and we have sought to straighten things out before the big committee meeting.

The situation has been as follows - largely among the hill colleges there is support of my position. These are the people who I have been working closely with and who I have been highly involved and connected with. All together there is myself and five others on the committee, however one of these is Josh himself who acts, or wants to be seen to act, as someone bringing people together - he would want to build common ground and consensus with others rather than simply ruling plans out.

Things get a bit more complicated when it comes to the town colleges. The five river colleges had their societies set up by Matt and are so fully behind him and fully supportive of his plan. I have not wasted time in trying to chip off support there. The three seafront colleges Matt approached and were thoroughly charmed and persuaded by him. They have lent their votes to him but they could well waver so it was here that I had many meetings to try and gain influence. The two marketplace colleges don't know what to make of it all, but seemed shocked by the lack of due process about it all.

So all these meetings went on through the week and I think that by the end I had managed to bring around the three seafront colleges. That would give us nine votes, a majority.

So it came to the meeting. I was ready to fight my corner, but the way it began confused me and left me...well you'll see:

Josh began, as someone relatively neutral in the dispute. He said that it had been wrong to push onto the committee big decisions without warning, and that what the incident had exposed was the weakness of the committee as a decision making body. There was no constitution, no way to elect a President, no formal process of composing an Agenda. Now that we were becoming more established we would have to become both more considered and formal in our leadership structure. I heartily approved of this intervention of Josh's and Matt actually made an apology for springing his plan on everyone without warning.

So, Josh said, before we consider any matters of substance, we have to regularise our structures. It was not easy, he said, but he had reproduced for us the standard constitution for a Dunwich Student Society. We voted to adopt it unanimously. 'Here comes the awkward part,' said Josh, 'we have to elect a President. Now, I don't want this to be a rehash of our previous dispute with Barry and Matt rancorously fighting it out. So it is with reluctance that I am offering myself for the position.' I looked across at Matt. I imagined that he would stand for President, despite it all. He wasn't going to give up on his plan so easily. Matt opened his mouth: 'I support Josh' he said. Since I trusted Josh, it didn't occur to me to stand myself and Josh was elected unanimously.

'Now,' said Josh, 'to appoint officers. To replace me at Cromwell College I appoint Hannah as the college rep, and she can also be Secretary with all those coloured pens she has. So one position remains, the Treasurer. I am picking Matt as the Treasurer.' I wasn't pleased but it made sense to try and keep Matt happy, lest he throw his toys out of the pram and cause more damage. 'Excellent,' said Josh. 'Now we have sorted all that we can proceed with the main business.'

Matt cleared his throat. 'There is one thing we have to do first,' he said. 'To regularise an anomaly. Take a look around. Everyone now has an officially recognised position. Except for Barry. He has no role. In fact, I'm not entirely sure what he's doing as part of this committee.'

I gaped. So this was how it was to go, I was going to be chucked out of the HH Society that I had built. Matt hadn't needed to be President, all he needed was approval of his plan - all he had needed to do was to support Josh who did want to be President, although he protested not to, and then in return he could put his plan into action. They had arranged it all between them behind the scenes and now I had no part in it. I don't know what I expected,

to somehow roam free as a revered founder. But it wasn't to be - I
was shut down.

I gathered my papers in silence to leave the room. I should have
been angry. I should have been raging and fighting and threatening
to set up a rival HH society. I should tear them all up - they have
sucked out the life from me and chewed me up and spat me out.
But instead I felt so terribly tired inside and wanted to just lie down
and rest and get away from these people consuming each other to
get ahead and to get their own way. It was all so distasteful and
pointless to me. They've made their choice - I think it will be so
much the worse for them and the whole thing will fall apart in their
hands. But it has passed beyond me now and it will do me no good
to grasp after it.

The worst thing of it all is that it has robbed me of my joy in
HH. I just feel really down and sad all the time. In all the conflict
and student politics I have lost the wonder. I just want to get away
from this place now.

Anyway...despite all this...I'm looking forward to you arriving in
a couple of weeks for the visit. It's actually been five years since
we've seen each other - will we even recognise each other?

B.

***

Cromwell College,
Dunwich, DW1 3EF
15/06/90

Dear Enid,
After being removed from the leadership of the Hoshi-Henro
Society it seemed as if nothing worse could happen to me. But twin
disasters have been visited upon me and now things are looking a
bit tricky.

First - I have failed my end of year exams. It is perhaps not
surprising with the play and chasing after Ellie and setting up the
city-wide societies. I didn't fail by much, but that isn't what counts.

I either have to retake the year or to drop out. It's all very disappointing, but not as much as it could be because...

Second - Ellie is leaving. Recently she had an ugly break up with Matt (I like to think because she is disgusted with the way he treated me) and now she simply wants to move on from Dunwich. I met her for a coffee and she said that she's come to hate the small-minded place. In September she will be transferring to the University of Inverness (far away) to continue the second year of her degree. Thing is, she's invited me to transfer up there with her. As I've been removed from my course AND from the HH group there is really nothing keeping me here so I thought I might as well go and start again with her. They don't have a physics department there but I could do something else.

It sounds strange, but two terrible things - failing and Ellie leaving, could actually lead to AMAZING - me getting to have what I wanted all along and had almost given up on - being with Ellie. In fact, she is nothing less than inviting me to be hers. Confusing times - with some decisions to make.

I can't believe that you'll be here next week. What will happen?

B.

***

Cromwell College,
Dunwich, DW1 3EF
30/06/90

Dear Enid,
Sorry. That's the first thing I should say, I suppose. I'm sorry for how things went when you visited. Looking back I should have expected it - to pitch you into the morass of my life was only to release more chaos.

For what it's worth I do recognise now that you were right and I'm sorry that the visit turned into one long argument. You are right: I have lost focus. I came here to build a RAD and got distracted with relationships and trying to set up an organisation. I get that now.

You'll be pleased that I've looked into it and by doing a remedial summer course I'll be able to stay on for the second year of physics - and this time stick to the aim of building a RAD. It will mean that I won't be able to travel with you this summer as I hoped, but it will be worth it. I'll also, naturally, let go all the things about the societies and Ellie. However painful it is, they don't lie in the direction I want to go - to glory.

Despite our sharp words there were some parts of your visit that I'll always remember with fondness and laughter. In particular: when you turned up at our college HH society meeting in full battle gear and holding your spacelance. When Matt saw you I think he pooped himself in terror - it certainly smelt like it. 'But you're...' he began, a look of stupefaction on his face. And when you just replied 'Real.' Classic. It cracked me up, it really did. And then Ellie wasn't entirely sure if you were my girlfriend or not and couldn't tell if she felt jealous or not. Good times.

I hope that you find what we hope for in those mountains this summer. I liked the way you put it: 'a breeze of fresher air, coming down the rock strewn path and up forested hill, the smell of spring bursting sharply, the reflection of starlight on the mere behind.'

With love
Barry

***

14 Thresham Street
Dunwich, DW1 5TP
14/07/90

Dear Enid,
I've had to move out of College for my summer remedial course. I'm looking forward to being about to focus on learning without all of the other student activities here for the summer. There are a lot of tourists though!

Do you really think you are heading towards a genuine portal this time? Past experience would suggest that perhaps this rumour too will evaporate when examined. But of course it could be the real deal. We won't know until you investigate. The mountains and scenery certainly sound impressive and more than ever I wish that I was there with you- but don't worry, I won't get distracted again!

I can't believe that my first year at university is already over. It has certainly been an eventful year. And to think, two more years of undergrad and then I'll start my PhD and through that actually get onto making a RAD - maybe say two years into the PhD. So, four years from now it could actually be happening! I know you think that you'll find this portal, this path to the stars, but I'm not so sure. I mean, it's probably a myth or wishful thinking. But of course, you must continue on your quest.

Now that I'm able to concentrate a bit better on the material it's all coming into focus and I think that I'll easily pass the assessment at the end of the six weeks. Not that I'm going to relax or take any chances. Every night I head back to study, and for most of the weekend as well, because if I blow this chance I'll have to retake the entire year and add one more year to the total before we can get that RAD.

Love Barry

***

14 Thresham Street,
Dunwich, DW1 5TP
30/07/90

Enid,

You say that you have found something - a definite something - a shifting portal. That it's only there some of the time. 'Up the hill in the crease of the rock strewn path, a breeze blowing down, smelling of something long-forgotten.' But when you got to the top it had vanished. Most strange. You'll have to investigate more fully. Of course, I don't really believe it and want to examine it myself, but what can I say, I am training to be a scientist after all.

That work of mine is still continuing and I am beginning to get a sense of the beauty of numbers and the elegance of the equations. I

want to write them out for you but I know you won't appreciate it -
I know a lost cause when I see it.

Write soon! Tell me what you discover in the folds and hollows of
those mountains.
B.

***

14 Thresham Street
Dunwich, DW1 5TP
12/08/90

Dear Enid,
I liked your postcard but it was very enigmatic. Only you would
send something like that with a single word: Cetastra! What do you
mean by it?

My course is almost over now, so I will have about a month left
of the holidays to fill. Should I follow you over to Central Europe?
Or should I get a summer job? Or just a chance to take a rest after
this crazy year. I haven't decided yet. Anyway, the test is in a few
days so I need to get back to revising.

B.

***

14 Thresham Street,
Dunwich, DW1 5TP
30/08/90

Dear Enid,
I haven't heard from you in a while and I am starting to get a little
worried. I know I'm probably being over-protective, but the
absolute worst things sometimes flit through my mind and I'm
scared for you. But I know you're probably fine and that there's
some perfectly rational explanation for you not writing - most likely
involving you having too much fun to have time to write.

Unless-

Unless of course the reason you haven't written is because you
found it. What you were looking for this whole time. Is that even
possible?

Write soon. Please.
Barry

***

14 Thresham Street
Dunwich, DW1 5TP
10/09/90

Dear Enid,
Where are you? Please write.
Barry

***

14 Thresham Street,
Dunwich, DW1 5TP
12/09/90

Dear Enid,
Your mother has written to me. She says that you are dead. But it
can't be true.

She says that there were reports of an American girl gone
missing in the mountains. That they found your bag and some
clothes - that you must have fallen into a crevasse or mountain lake.
That it's too late now to hold out any hope.

She says that they're having a funeral for you next week. I don't
know what they'll put in the coffin. She's invited me to the funeral.
But I'm not going. Before term starts I'm going to search the
mountains. Perhaps you're lost and alone somewhere, trapped.
They wouldn't know how to find you like I would. I have to do it.

Barry

***

30/09/90

Dear Enid,

I had to return in the end for the start of term. I know that's what you'd want me to do.

I wasn't able to find you. I looked everywhere that you described - I was glad of all the details you gave - but couldn't find you. I don't know why but I was convinced that I would be able to do it.

Perhaps the reason you can't be found is not because you are dead. Perhaps it is because you no longer tread this earth but the path of the stars. That you have been changed into the likeness of reality. I couldn't find the portal but you did say that it is shifting - maybe it has gone from the place now forever.

The students are returning here now - or arriving for some of them - and the chill of autumn is starting to spread across the marshes and streets once more. But all I can think about are those tracks on the mountains.

B.

***

14 Thresham Street,
Dunwich, DW1 5TP
16/10/90

Dear Enid,

Your Mum has asked me to stop writing - all your post/mail is being sent on to her and it's distressing her. It's true, I don't know who I'm writing to any more, or if I'm even writing to anyone.

What I do know, with growing conviction over the past month, is that you are not dead. I think that you did find that path to the stars, and that you have entered into the world of Hoshi-Henro.

I read again those last lines that you wrote 'up the hill in the crease of the rock strewn path, a breeze flowing down, smelling of something long-forgotten.' I want to brand them onto my soul.

I may have missed my chance to be with you now on your adventure, but I will join you as soon as I can. Now more than ever I will dedicate myself to building the Reality Alteration Device so that I can follow where you have led. I will do it - it is what my life shall be about.

Then we will finally be together in the world of Hoshi-Henro, amongst the stars, away from this weary world.

Barry

***

20/10/90
Enid - I miss you.

***

31/10/90
Enid?

A WEEK IN THE LIFE OF AMY WU, SUMMER 1994, DUNWICH

Friday 10 June, lunchtime

When I was a little girl I heard a story. It was about the Prince who travels to a far country to rescue the one that he loves; the Prince who lays down his own life to win the heart of the one he seeks. The Prince of my heart. For a long time I believed in this Prince, that he could make me his princess, just like Diana. All through my girlhood I hoped he would find me, and as a teenager waited for love's true kiss. Then I grew up. Now I don't know what I believe. I still feel the pull, the attraction of the fairy tale with the Prince. But my experience of life teaches me that it cannot be true. Despite a lot of searching (believe me) I have only found faint resemblances to that Prince. Most likely he is a dream, a mirage, a fantasy. I need to come to terms with reality. But it isn't easy and I often slip into the old ways of thinking...

We were waiting in the queue of the sandwich shop, Sammys, and I was talking with Caroline, one of the other interns, about the others.

'Peter is quite nice,' said Caroline. 'He has that floppy hair.'

'But what about the nose? Do you think anyone can even get close enough to his mouth for a kiss?'

'Yeah there is the nose. How about you?'

'I definitely have the hots for Pascal. Those dreamy brown eyes. The curly hair. Every time I speak to him I can't help but blush. He-'

'Sshh, they're just ahead of us in the queue.'

There the two of them were, just ahead of us. They were facing forwards and had not noticed us. They were talking, rather loudly.

'What's going on with you?' asked Peter.

'Nothing much, mainly concentrating on my poetry.'

'I know last time we talked you were feeling warm towards Amy...'

'Amy,' he spat. 'Don't talk to me about her. That pig-faced, whiney, ignorant toad. I try to have as little to do with her as possible.'

'I don't feel like sandwiches,' I said and rushed out. Caroline trailed
behind me as I marched along the street. 'How dare he!'
'That was out of order.'
'And I don't look like a pig do I?'
'I think your nose is cute.'
'He's a monster and I hate him.'
'I know what will cheer you up. Book basement...now. I'll pick us
up some lunch on the way.'
'Alright.'

Arylhadon's Books is on Thresham Street and is a maze of little
rooms and crooked book lined corridors. Cobweb infested corners
and torn armchairs squeeze beside tottering towers of cut price
textbooks and faded gilt collectors editions. It was the sort of place
to get lost in.

The book basement is where books go to die. On the bottom floor
is one giant open space filled with giant vats sunk into the ground
and filled to overflowing with unsold books. You could fill a black
plastic sack for fifty pence. The great sea of books is criss-crossed
with narrow raised walkways, so the only way to look for books is
to kneel down and extend downwards into the books on your
elbows. This is why we came, because as people (ok guys)
descended into the morass of literature to search it was the perfect
opportunity to assess their arses.

Caroline and I had dragged an old vinyl sofa to the perfect angle to
watch, and there we ate our sandwiches.
'A 5,' said Caroline, looking at a bottom raised upwards, whose
owner strained down.
'That's mean. He's at least a 7,' I said.
'I have perfect taste,' she said. 'The arse score will match the
hotness of his face.' This was one of our contentions, the holistic
hotness, where every aspect of a person must be in balance.
'Look out. He's getting up,' I said. 'Haha look at those high
cheekbones.'

'Crap.'
'You have got terrible taste. What good are your bum scores if they don't give us a clue to the overall hotness of the guy?'
'My score does not lie. Listen to me. There'll be something wrong with him, some screwed up corner of his life.'
'Isn't there with all of them?'
'Do you know who does lie? You.'
'Where's this coming from?' I asked.
'You do still like Pascal. Even after what he said.'
'Absolutely not. I'll prove it to you too. I am so over him that I am ready to launch into someone else.'
'Who do you think you're kidding,' said Caroline.

'What about that one?' I asked, indicating another posterior with my eyes.
'8,' she said.
'4,' I replied. We waited for the big reveal. As he stood up we saw a craggy face topped with white hair. 'You are seriously off your game today.'
'That is - I don't know what to say.'
'You have secret crushes on pensioners? Come on, admit it!'
'I clearly have a dirty mind. Come on, let's do another. Give me a chance to redeem myself.
'Fine, one more. But we better be getting back soon, we're already way past our lunch break.'
'That one,' said Caroline

'Ooooh,' I said, looking closely '10,' I announced.
'10? No way.'
'Yes way.'
'Do you realise what you're saying? That you cannot imagine or conceptualise any better arse than that one. That any arse you encounter will be a let-down after this peak of perfection. That this may well be the best bum in the whole world. Do you understand, are you sure? A 10 is not to be given lightly.'
'Yes, I am sure,' I said after a moment of further scrutiny.

'Then there's only one thing for you to do,' she said. 'You better grab it before it slips away.'
'What, now?'
'When else. Quick whilst you have the chance or live a life of regret.'
'I don't know…'
'Now now now,' she said.

I got up and quietly took up position behind him. I stretched out my hand and touched. I pulled and rolled between my fingers a wad of flesh, in a pinch of passion. He jumped, startled, and turned around, his lips twisted in surprise.
'What!...Amy?'
'Barry?' It was the guy from the undergrad course who had been into that sci-fi show. I hadn't reckoned on knowing the guy.
'What were you, what was-?'
'Just my way of saying hello,' I lied. 'You know me, crazy kooky Amy.'
'Oh ok,' he said.
'What are you doing these days?' I asked, trying to move the conversation on from the bum pinching.
'Coming to the end of my second year of PhD. You?'
'Intern at the Centre for Criminology…it must have been a few years since I've seen you, right? We got to head now but let's catch up sometime.'
'Yes a cup of tea or-'
'I know, come with us tonight, we're going out, a group of us. You must it's the perfect chance or it'll never happen. We're going to the dance barn.'
'I don't-'
'Meet us at the footpath near Causeway Bridge. The south side. At 8pm.'
'But-'
'Got to go,' I said, breezing out with Caroline.

We left quickly.

'You like him,' Caroline said. I didn't know how to reply because I did.

Friday afternoon
At the back of the Criminology Centre was a small yard. It might have once been a garden or delivery area but had become a mass of sprouting weeds from concrete paving slabs, until several of last year's interns had decided to intervene. The stalks and tendrils were cut back and in their place appeared a small garden. It was constantly supplemented by whoever took the fancy, filling with: a deckchair, a few stools, a square of fake grass, various candles in jam jars, cushions, a stack of tartan blankets, a barbeque, a plastic table, a row of roses in pots.

On Fridays we quit work early to come out here.

This time, I was there first with Caroline at about four and we watched the others emerge through our sunglasses.

The sun gently baked the paving slabs. The wind tugged at the wispy ends of weeds poking from the clefts. Ants hurried on their looping paths. Overhead clouds slouched past and the cry of gulls echoed through the narrow streets and passages.

The long golden rays and thick shadows danced lazily around as people came out gulping the warm air before sinking into the buzz of life.
'I could sit like this forever,' I said. I was wearing my work shirt, pleated skirt hitched up for max exposure to the sun. Wrap around sunglasses on my eyes.
'It's so drouzifying,' said Caroline yawning.
'I could spend the rest of my life looking at the little cracks in the slabs,' I said.
'Nothing can disturb us now,' said Caroline.
'Hang it all, I can't stop thinking about Pascal.'
'I don't blame you, he can be obnoxious.'

'What's the word I'm looking for, it's on the tip of my tongue.'
'Pretentious?'
'No...er...conceited.'
'All of the above,' said Caroline. 'I know what'll take your mind off it all. Come with me to Saxmundham, they've got a movie showing. Four Weddings.'
'How many times have you seen it already?'
'It doesn't matter, I'll go one more time.'
'We've got Natalie's big dinner on Sunday, remember?'
'Forgot about that.'
'Next week then.'
'Alright.'

We soaked back into the sun bliss again only stirring when Natalie brought the beers.
'So, who have you got your eye on?' asked Caroline.
'Talking about boys again?' she said. 'Seriously you two need to branch out and stop defining yourselves by the men in your lives. Open your eyes to this glorious afternoon. Can't we talk about something else?'
'Sure,' I said. 'Didn't you say you were thinking of quitting the internship? What's up with that?'
'I'm not staying,' she said. 'I thought I could do it but I just can't. I'm not made for all these investigations.'
'They can really suck, you're right,' said Caroline.
'I thought it sounded exciting at the time,' she continued. 'But it is such an almighty bore fest. Looking through all the records and doing all the grunt work. No way. I'm getting out.'
'Do you think you'll stay here long?' Caroline asked me. 'At the Centre?'
'Yes, I like it,' I said. 'I think I'll stay for the long haul.'
'But what is it that you like about it?'
'The searching and the grinding. The not knowing if a trail will suddenly open up if you grind away at the evidence and crunch through, and then it does and it's as if a whole hidden world has been unveiled. Or it doesn't and it's a dead end and then you have to chip away again at another part of the picture but you know

you've got closer to the truth by ruling something out. I suppose it's a passion for the truth, for finding it and upholding it. For finding the real story behind all the show. That's what this place is about and that's what I want to do.'

'You made it sound real fancy,' said Natalie. 'But day to day its making carbon copies of lists of addresses and searching for names in registers and writing official information request letters. So dull.'

'But it all builds up to a greater whole,' I said.

'But not too much to skive off early on a Friday afternoon…'

'Let's not get carried away.'

We settled once again into the comfortable haze.

At 5pm a few people came out, the work day officially over. Pascal was one of them.

'Amy,' he said. 'I hope you've remembered to file those case reports.'

'Of course I haven't forgotten. I'll do them in their proper time.'

'The deadline is next week.'

'Exactly. Plenty of time.'

'I think that–'

'Look you're not my boss,' I said.

'Fine,' he replied and sat down beside Natalie.

'What we doing tonight Amy?' Natalie said. 'I'm hoping for some candle-lit escapades, cellars and rooftop champagne and imported ice and rootin' tootin' dancing and fit boys in tuxes and bodices and mysteries and gin palaces and late-night skinny dips in the sea.'

'We're going to the dance barn at the edge of town,' I said.

'Nothing too wild. Not this time.'

'She's invited this major geek we bumped into today,' Caroline said.

'She got it going for him.'

'He's an old friend,' I said.

'Really though it's just his bum that she fancies. She thinks it is perfect.'

'Seldom have I the chance to see the perfect arse,' said Natalie.

'Count me in.'

'Pascal, do you want to come?'

'Loath as I am to miss rear of the year, I have tickets to a poetry reading,' said Pascal.
'What sort of thing, you mean like Ted Hughes?' asked Caroline.
'Not that derivative stuff, something more experimental. This new poet musician called Josh. He deconstructs the form itself.'
'Sounds rubbish,' I said. 'There's a reason that Larkin and Hughes are popular, it's because they write actual poetry not messing around with postmodern hijinks.'
'When did you start liking poetry?' said Pascal.
'I have a general interest in topics that stimulate the intellect,' I said. 'Though as a rule I don't go in for poetry.'
'You don't have the poetic temperament,' said Pascal. 'You wouldn't enjoy it tonight.'
'We've got plenty enough to look forward to,' I said. 'But first, we need to charge ourselves up with sunlight so we can spill it out at everyone through the night.'

Friday evening
The street lamp lighters were out as we crossed over Greyfriars bridge, my silvery stilettos slipping on the cobbles. The spires of the town stood in silhouette, an assortment of spikes pinning and folding the splashes of orange into night. Before we had left I had changed into my shoes, silver-pink metallic skirt and sequin halterneck, so that I felt like a sexy party robot. Natalie had a floral babydoll dress with doc martens, Caroline leopard print pantsuit, it wasn't her best look.

The evening's woodsmoke clung to us as the night's coldness drew its shawl around us and I breathed in deeply and was filled with a sense of energy. The night was mine and lay open for me. Barry was waiting by the causeway and I gathered him into the group as we walked on the path beside the river. The salt marshes on either side greyed into twilight and the town became a cluster of warm dots and holes, the coast beyond a sharp cliff of darkness. The path rose from the riverbank, and we talked of the bands that evening, the animals we thought we heard in the undergrowth, the roosting

of birds. The path meandered around fusty gorse bushes and
tattered groups of trees, breaking up into rivulets, joining together,
on long loops. Until we cut through a hedgerow, reaching the lane,
and beyond it the farm.

One of the barns often lay empty and so the farmers let it out to
performing groups. We mainly went for the dancing, though the
beer wasn't bad. Whilst the sticky floored clubs in South Street
were full of students and American tourists, this place, on the edge
of town was real and gritty and cool. Plus there was no chance of
pulling an eighteen year old by mistake.

By now the sky was diesel; warm gaslight was streaming out of the
doors of the barn; the growl and strum of pounding music sped
through the entrance and a wave of it met us as we entered. A song
was concluding and the hot air filled with cheers.

The guitars and trumpets flared as they prepared for the next song
of their set. The drums rolled. The band broke into a rowdy bass
line and something roused in me as the rocking vocals kicked in, as
I left Barry to fend for himself, quickly leaping into the assembling
fray

The music brought me into the present: moving back and forth,
left and right with quickness; stepping and pounding and stomping
and clapping; my brain hums with the hormones of action and
reward and I am lifted far above myself, or rather, I find in me the
life which is now unlocked and released and pours out in a raging
torrent.

I feel a soaring wildness as pure life flows through me and the beat
rouses my sleeping soul. Here my bones become charged with
electricity and I feel like a coil about to burst out. The pulsating
grabs me and throws me about, magnetised and drawn into the roar
of existence itself. I am raised higher as instinct itself is channelled,
the brain short circuited and discursive thought bypassed to
experience the present moment in all its richness, which rationality

cannot define or contain. In this barn is the boiling rhythm and insistent drum which shakes me into action.

I turn and twist and jump and shout, wave and sidle and hop and drag and bop and grind and slide and pull and push and flap and pump and hold and stand with hands high in the air. And I feel connected to everyone else who is here, one people, one movement, one spirit. Here I give myself into this spirit of the night, to be used by her hands as I channel something elemental, unadorned, prehistoric. This is exulting in a body fully alive. This is living. Life is good.

I was not surprised Barry had not joined in. After several songs I sought him out. He was at the side, in the bar area, holding a bottle of beer as if it were a teddy bear. He had not drunk any.

'This all seems a little uncontrolled to me,' he said.
'Dancing is a form of communication,' I shouted, close to his ear. It was loud so I couldn't be sure he had heard.
'Not one I have ever learned. And it's a little hard to catch up with all this noise. Isn't it all just a stand in for...you know?'
'What? Sex you mean? It can be, sure, but there's more to it than that.'
'I think I'll go and stand outside. I should be able to see Orion and the Pleiades right now. It will be nice and quiet and cool out there. This is like an assault.'
'Come on,' I say, and grabbed his hand.

He's shy and I like that. He only resists a little, before I sweep him into the flow, but I have to show him how to do everything. He doesn't know what to do, how to move, he is thinking about it all. I hold his hand, get him to follow me. When I press his hand in mine he looks at my eyes and opens his mouth slightly. He never looked me in the eyes before.

I get him to join in for a while until we are both red faced and hot and very thirsty, and then we grab a drink and go out. Beside the barn are rectangles of hay and fire pits and the light and beat leaks out, and sitting here it is easier to talk. We slump into a circle a little distance from the barn - me and Barry, joined by Natalie and Caroline and Peter.

'I survived it,' he said. He wore a proud smile.
'You might have even enjoyed it a little bit,' I said.
'Maybe,' he said.

Peter chucks some more wood on the smouldering heap. The light from the fire licks our faces. In the shadowy bushes at the edge of vision dark figures moved about, pissing or screwing or dealing.

'What you working on?' asked Peter.
'PhD,' he said. 'Two years through now.'
'Rad man,' Peter said.
'Yeah you must be glad you're ripping through it,' said Natalie.
'Well actually my research isn't going so well...I've got stuck and I don't know what to do...I promised...I've got to make it but I just can't, there's no way. It's impossible. I don't know what to do.'
'Don't worry. Everything's going to be ok,' I said.
'Yeah, take a chill pill,' said Caroline.
'Or better, some of this,' said Natalie. She passed around a spiff which Barry did not take, and the conversation moved on.

Barry did a couple more dances through the night, but if he wanted to stay outside I let him. I wasn't going to get distracted from the dancing. Once when I went out to him on the hay bales I sat on his lap. He was too shocked to push me off.

Eventually the night came to a close. We couldn't find Peter, Caroline reckoned he had gone off with some girl, so the rest of us started to stagger away from the barn.

Unsteadily we climbed the stile, bumping into one another in the darkness of the overhanging trees. As we emerged from the undergrowth, the entire city was spread before us in the moonlight,

the low marsh between us leading our eyes to the bricks and domes
and bells of Dunwich.
'I need a piss,' said Caroline.
'Squat down in the undergrowth, no one can see. No one would
care anyway,' said Natalie.
'By myself?'
'Fine, I'll stay and keep watch,' said Natalie. Barry and I continued
on.

He led us down, through shadowed reed-beds and the raised levees;
pools of water and trenches and bends of still water. My shoes sunk
into the mud and I carried them. The night creatures were startled
and we heard their noises as we tramped on through. But as we
walked on, we seemed to be getting no closer to the city. Though
we had been walking some time. Finally the path was halted by a
great trough of water that we could not pass, and he sat down on a
damp bank.
'We're stuck in the swamps,' he said. 'I've been this way many
times. Even in the dark. But I don't seem to be able to…'
'Look I wouldn't mind sleeping here but it's bloody cold,' I said.
There would be a frost when the sun rose. 'Can you find any way
out?'
'It just doesn't look the same,' she said.
'Do you mean that you are lost?'
'You have no idea how lost I am,' he said, and his face suddenly
scrunched up all ugly.
'Sshh,' I said as I calmed him, stroking his hair. 'I'm here. I'm right
next to you to help.'

I raised his head to mine and kissed him, gently at first, and then he
responded greedily. As if he was trying to suck out of me
something he didn't have. When Natalie and Caroline arrived we
stopped, and I held his hand all the way back to the city as he gave
me bashful glances.

Sunday evening
Natalie liked to throw dinner parties and insisted we made an event
of it. I'm more of a houseparty girl, but can appreciate it. Barry
wasn't keen to join in.
'If we're together now, we got to do things together,' I said.
'We're together?'
'I thought we were.'
'Yes sure, I mean, of course we are. The idea is just a little new to
me.'
'You better get used to it.'
'I'll try.'
'So you're coming tonight.'
'Yes, of course, naturally.

The guest list: Me and Barry. Natalie and her housemates, Cloris
and Hannah. Caroline and Peter and Hugo. Gail and Pascal. Ten in
all, five from the Centre, a squeeze in her narrow terraced house.
I wore a white t-shirt beneath a strappy black dress. The others
mostly wore sweatshirts and jeans, except Caroline and Natalie.
Caroline had on a denim vest and Natalie neon pink hotpants.

They had patched together three tables through the lounge and
dining room, and in the corner stood an army of wine bottles,
pouring freely, warming quickly - mouths and hearts. Conversation
whirled around as Natalie poured us some drinks
'Really? I actually cried when I heard John Smith had died.'
'Never mind that, who is it that you think will be the next Labour
leader.'
'I'd like it to be Margaret Beckett, Labour's never had a female
leader...but it's fairly unlikely, she's not that popular...'
'I don't understand why Gordon Brown hasn't stood. He's the
serious candidate.'
'Let's face it, none of them can compete with Tony Blair. Look at
that smile.'
'Like a crocodile.'
'Don't be ridiculous...'

'Sit down sit down, said Natalie, herding us into our seats. 'Sit tight because the starters are coming.' She brought out small bowls of a chilli and grapefruit and carrot salad tossed with fresh coriander and topped with a sprinkle of chopped dates.

I was sitting with Barry on one side and Pascal on the other. Opposite me was Caroline. Further down, near Barry were Peter and Hugo. From down the table I heard the drift of a football conversation:
'My Dads going over to the US for the world cup soon...yeah he won't let me come.'
'Who do you think will win?'
'Italy are looking good…'

Unwilling to be subsumed into a football conversation, I set up a topic myself:
'I read a book the other day, the End of History. Now the cold war is over we are finally entering an era of peace and prosperity.'
'I'm surprised that you are taken in with such fallacious nonsense,' said Pascal.
'Ooohhh I feel a Amy Debate coming on,' Caroline said as I blushed.
'And what is so famous about my discussions?'
'They get a little involved. Epic perhaps is the right word.'
'Better to admit you are wrong on the off,' said Pascal. 'It's classic Whig view of history stuff, all proved wrong.'
'There has been no such proof,' I said. 'On the contrary, I will prove to you that the world is getting better in every way.'
'You're such an optimist Amy,' said Caroline.
'No no,' I said. 'It's all real, not wishful thinking.'
'You're looking on the bright side?'
'I wouldn't call it the bright side. I'm no idealist. I'm looking at things as they are. The world is becoming a better place all the time. The final Russian troops have left East Germany. The world is at peace once again.'
'Are you kidding?' said Pascal. 'As we speak the Rwandan civil war is raging, and we are discovering that a genocide has been

committed. Did you miss that piece of news? The world is not a
pretty place.'
'I know about that. But in South Africa Nelson Mandela has just
been elected President and the era of racism and oppression is
rolling back forever, never to return.'

We continued the debate as I held forth on the wonders of travel
and technological advancement, and he gave a catalogue of
conflicts through the world, until Natalie hushed us so we could
gawp at her efforts in the kitchen, bringing out the main course.

Huge bulbs of roasted garlic and fennel and charred sweet bitter
orange slices piled up and slathered with mustard and butter.

Salty crispy roasted potatoes and parsnips with garlic and thyme
and a sticky caramel sauce.

Curls of red chicory enclosing balls of spiced sausage meat rolled in
honey

Creamed leek and asparagus with lemon rind.

Bacon fried cauliflower cheese topped with an entire disc of brie.

Salt baked slabs of rosemary chicken with thick wine and
mushroom infused gravy.

For a time we concentrated on the food; speaking of it, eating it,
praising it, deciding our favourite fish, reaching for more.

'I don't understand,' said Caroline. 'Surely this food itself is proof
of the goodness of the world.'
'Step on the scales and say that,' said Pascal.
'Amy, go get him,' said Caroline, and we started up again. The ideas
that flung between us increased in speed, rapid shots catapulted
into ideological defences.
'Environmental degradation is spreading.'

'So is education and democracy. Poverty rates are in freefall around the globe.'
'Morality is degrading and family life corrupting.'
'Princess Diana.'
'That is not an argument.'
'Yes it is, just look at her and her dresses. Did you even see the safety clip one?'
'Fine. Prince Charles.'
'Grunge fashion is officially dead. (By the way Pascal, 1993 called, it wants its plaid jacket back.)'
'IRA bombings.'
'Bill Clinton.'
'Noel Edmunds.'
'The Channel Tunnel has opened, bringing friendship and croissants across the sea.'
'Also snails.'

As the argument grew ever more heated I looked at Barry. I don't think he had said anything the whole time. He seemed to recede in the conversation, to drift far out on a distant tide. He sometimes seemed to be paying attention to the conversation to the left, sometimes to the right, but hopping from one to the other and never making any contribution other than facial expressions. He was disconnected. Isolated.

'We need to end this debate or we'll be here forever,' said Caroline. 'I will adjudicate. You have both put forward excellent points, but Amy of course is the winner.'
'Thank you,' I said, toasting her.
'You're only saying that because she's your friend,' Pascal said.
'What terrible slander,' said Caroline. 'She wins because the world is both beautiful and brutal and the balance between the two is entirely subjective. If we have to pick one, let's at least pick the happy one.'
'It's all fairy tales and nonsense,' said Pascal, and got up from the table with a jolt.
'Has he actually left?' asked Caroline.

'Double win for me!'
'You goading minx!'

Natalie brought out the desert. It turned out that Pascal had gone
to help her, and then swapped places so he wouldn't have to endure
my gloating. The deserts were roasted pears covered with spun
sugar and with a bit of ice cream on the side. Coffee followed
immediately after, but by now everyone was full and bloated and
lethargic and the conversation floated away from each of us as we
became more relaxed and comfortable.

It was time to leave. Pascal only said to me: 'Did you send the case
reports?' and then left.

I took Barry's hand in mine as we stepped into the street.
'You didn't say much?'
'I don't really keep up with the news. In any case, I didn't feel that I
fit in.'
'Of course you did.'
'That's not what I meant. I mean...I don't cut much of a figure
compared to Pascal. He was clearly into you.'
'Come off it, we were arguing the whole time.'
'He couldn't take his eyes off you.'
'Don't worry about that...he's the most annoying person I've ever
met.'
'Ok,' he said quietly.
'Do you want to come over to mine?' I asked.
'No it's ok, I just feel a bit down, I think I'll just head home.'

Monday evening

I was cooking Barry some pasta. He doesn't seem to be eating
properly and at times looks skeletal, so I invited him around to feed
him up. My housemates were out so we sat in the narrow dining
galley by ourselves.
'What do you want to do tonight?'

'I don't know, I'm tired - something relaxing?'
'I've got the perfect thing,' I said. 'I found out that the Middle Common Room of your college is having an event. It's your own college, your own level, the MCR. It's perfect.'
'I don't know. What sort of event?
'You need to get out there,' I said. 'Come up and I'll show you what it is.'
'That's a little ominous,' he said, but he followed me up the creaking stairs to my room anyway.

'It's a costume party!' I said, once I had seated him on the bed.
'I don't know, it's not really my thing. I tried the dinner party and tried my best but I don't want to put myself through that again. Maybe it's best if I don't go.'
'I know you like Hoshi-Henro, so I got us some costumes.'
'What do you mean?'
'I got some stuff we can dress up in.'

From the wardrobe I took out two perfect costumes, crisp and clean.
'I've got you Pequod. See the regulation grey, the blue trimming for his rank, even those details on the belt.'
'Wow, it's amazing. It's really accurate,' he said, touching it, 'and high quality too!'
'What can I say, I have a thing for cosplay. Now, here's the big choice for you - what about me in this costume? I have a few different coloured novelty wigs so I can be whoever you want...Eiko, Reiji, the Captain.'
'Not the Captain!'
'Any of the other three then. Whoever.'

He held the costume tenderly as if it were a baby

'I'll go to the bathroom and-'
'Just get changed here like me, it's nothing more than you can see at the swimming pool or beach.'
'I haven't been to a swimming pool for ten years.'

'But you've been to the beach, right? You live in a seaside town.'
'Technically a seaside city.'
'Stop evading.'
'I haven't managed to find my way to the beach yet.'
'In five years?'
'Yes.'
'That's it, I'm taking you, but not now. Now, you get changed.'

To be honest I wanted to see a bit more of that perfect arse, but only caught a glimpse as he trod off his trousers and wriggled into the new ones. When he took off his top I could see his ribs sticking out and I wanted to stroke each one. Once he was ready he straightened everything out and looked in the mirror. He smiled. All suited up, he really did look a lot like Pequod from the show, I don't know why I didn't notice it before.

'How did you get these anyway?'
'They're mine, left over from that pantomime you put on. I sorted my own costume myself.'
'Play not pantomime.'
'Yes that's what I meant. I am, or I was, a big fan of the show a few years back. Not so much now. There was a real craze for it whilst we were undergrads, wasn't there?'
'Did you ever come to those special meetings?'
'No, not me. I liked the show, and I even got up and about in your pantomime-'
'-Drama.'
'Yes drama. But that's all. It's a good TV show, and it caught a cultural moment but nothing more. The effects even look a bit crappy now.'
'The thing you have to understand is that it was more to me than a TV show.'
'You're one of those superfans aren't you?'
'No it's not that. It's different. I believe that the TV show is the reality and our lives are fabricated. Or something like that, it's what Enid taught me.'
'What am I meant to say to that?'

'If you think I'm crazy?'
'Everyone's a little crazy when you get to know them...and everyone has to believe in something…people believe in all kinds of weird stuff like reincarnation and crystals and Moses.'
'You sound like you're trying to persuade yourself.'
'You are nuts, that whole idea is nuts, but so long as it doesn't harm anyone and it makes you happy, I'm fine with it.'
'But it's not making me happy. It's making me miserable.'
'How so?'
'It's my research, for my PhD. I'm at the point of giving up, really. It seems that my central thesis is wrong. You see, I was to create a Reality Alteration Device that would provide a path into true reality, the world of Hoshi-Henro. But I just can't do it. My supervisor has given me the option to divert the research into a paper on the mirror mathematics, but if I take it up then it's admitting defeat. It'd be admitting that the whole idea of the RAD is wrong.'
'If it's wrong, just admit it. It's all meant to be part of the research, right. You've learnt and discovered something even through a dead-end.'
'But I can't because of Enid.'
'Who is this Enid? Was she your girlfriend or something.'
'No, she was more than that. She went missing, and...and I believe that she found a way to travel to the stars.'
'But if you just say you've found that no such path exists…'
'Then she must have died. And she can't have.'
'It's all looking a bit shaky to me.'
'It feels like all of life is about to fall apart. Or that I am. I don't know how much longer I can keep on going for.
'Barry you need to see a doctor.'
'No I...I just need some space, a chance to breathe, something to take my mind off it all so that...I'm too wrapped up in it all, that's all.'
'That's what I was saying Barry, you've got to get out of yourself. Now, come here, I've got to put my costume on. The skirt is very short.'

We didn't make it to the party that night.

Tuesday early morning
I left Barry sleeping in my bed, I would be back before he woke. I
often got up early to go swimming. Walking past early morning
wild garlic, gorse and sheep grazing on the meadows, it felt as if the
whole world was a present, new and shiny, opening itself for me.

The morning is early and clear and a little cold. It has that smell of
a chilly morning on a summers day is the scent of possibility...that
fresh brightness that speaks, saying 'the whole day is yours and shall
be as sweet and juicy and satisfying as a perfectly ripe peach.' Later
these first aromatics released by the plants will become
overwhelmed by the heaviness of the day's heat, overlaid with
tenderising asphalt,
sun baked skin, burnt layers of sky. But for now it felt like
absolutely anything could happen today, and that was wonderful.

The lido is by the river in the middle of Hook Green and is
hemmed around on three sides by changing cabins. The final side
faces the river itself, separated by a narrow strip of footway and
iron fence posts so that it is as if there were two pools side by side,
long and thin. The entrance was a rickety turnstile on the north side
with an old red bucket for the fee and an unchanging old man
sitting smoking with an unread novel. It is unheated. On summer
mornings it is perishingly cold.

In one of the empty cabins I folded up my dungarees and jacket
and put on my old bobbly black one piece for serious swimming.
Stepping out into the cold air I frill into goosebumps. The pool
before me is covered with a smooth sheen, the light bent and
warped by the water, a strange mirror. It is very blue, like the
morning sky, a piercing blue.

I jumped in and felt the shock of it, my body tingling and jolting as
the blood rushed inwards from the chill. I can feel every part of my

body. It seems as if I was not awake before, though I was walking and looking. Now through the cold water I had broken into a greater wakefulness and the world both seemed to hum and for the noise of my brain to subside.

I start to swim breast stroke gently, and the little lapping waves I make cut up the surface of the water, and the mirror-like surface is broken. The disturbances in the water curl and lick around me, massaging my body
The only sounds I hear are of the calming swish of water as it is delved away with my hands, of my own breathing and the pump of my blood. The joy of exercise, of rushing dopamine floods through me.

The sky is very big this close to the ground. It curves up in a vast arch and kisses the horizon. From the pool I can see the river beyond, running parallel to the pool, and beyond that, Greyfriars Pastures surrounding the college itself, the oldest in Dunwich. It stood worn by time, with cloisters and spire. I had been to some killer parties there, they have a bar in the cellars. They say that when the ancient Friars built their spire it was the same time Salisbury Cathedral was built, and the Friars made theirs to the same design only ensured their spire was a foot taller. Beyond the spire the sky is blue and faintly dusted with feathers of icing sugar clouds. The sun is low and glints of the rippling waters, at certain angles blinding. I feel connected to nature, to the world, subsumed within it, a part, a simple creature doing creaturely things.

Soon, others begin to join the pool and the lifeguard begins to give more attention, climbing aboard her tall chair. I recognise some of them; the speedy man in the red trunks and green goggles; the elderly woman who looks like she's past it but always dives in so elegantly; the dude with ripped muscles whose technique is so poor I always overtake him. As more people enter the waves become more rippled as their tracks cross and collide. The earlier peace is gone as we negotiate

Then a sight that I was unused to: Pascal entering wearing yellow swimming shorts. He gives me a nod as he eases himself in, and then he begins his splashing swim. With him there the pool seemed cramped, and he always seems to be on my tail, occasionally scraping me with his nails and generally being an oppressive presence. I tried to ignore him, but he was creating large waves and kept splashing into my eyes with his wide and ungainly crawl. He was fast though.

I was glad when he made to leave. I would have time for a few more lengths without him. I wondered who had told him about this place and ruined my perfect early morning fix. Standing at the edge of the pool dripping he beckoned me over.
'What is it?' I asked, leaning on the pool edge, his whole body towering above me.
'Have you sent in those case reports yet?'

Anger flared deep within me. How dare he bring that up again? Why did he have to keep on getting in my face, messing with my life. He was so infuriating.
'You are the most disagreeable person that I have ever met,' I said. He arched an eyebrow in reply, not even giving me an answer. My anger hardened into something else, something dangerous. In a quick movement of rage I reached up and pulled down his shorts.

His thing was small wrinkled and greyish. For half a second he stood frozen and then the lifeguard's whistle was blowing and he pulled them up as she shouted about nudity at the pool. His face was mashed up in anger he left without a word.

I laughed to myself - pity the person who ends up with that worm in their life. I did a couple more lengths to get it all out of my system.

Getting out, and casting all thoughts of Pascal aside, I was filled simultaneously by a tiredness and freshness. As I dried my hair I realised the whole day lay before me still. I was hungry, I would fix us up some food when I got back. Barry was waiting sleepily in my bed. Under the duvet he was warm and naked.

Tuesday morning
I hadn't seen Pascal at work. I think he has been avoiding me. I wouldn't mind seeing him. I've been practicing what sort of expression I should wear in the mirror. At the moment it's a tie between knowing contempt, smug confidence and utter pity. Actually I've been looking for him so as to try one of these out.

Unfortunately the Centre for Criminology is an easy place to hide.

It takes up several Georgian townhouses on Cowloe Street and has five levels, multiple staircases, a basement for records and an attic. It is entirely possible to move around from department to department in a circle or figure of eight and avoid meeting another staff member you want to avoid. But the Centre was unusual in many ways. The Centre for Criminology is probably unique in combining the work of an academic research centre with both a unit of private detectives and a comprehensive legal outfit. It is the place to go when you have a mystery which cannot be solved by anyone else, often through lack of Police interest. We provide services to individuals, companies and even sometimes the Government itself. If the truth of a matter is unclear, we are the ones who can uncover it, especially if nefarious illegal doings are involved.

My role as an intern covered lots of things from helping with the internal nail to doing the tea round. But at the moment it focused on the case reports. The case documents were produced by the lawyers in the legal department relating to a case and related to the investigation documents produced by the Investigations Department. But before they could be filed with the Dunwich magister and for the case to proceed, they had to be written into the standard pro forma of the city. The problem was that I was fed this teeming and overflowing mass of information and I had to order and synthesise them in the best way: forensic reports, psychological analyses, previous case law, call histories, interview transcripts. They all had to be fed in. Of course what many did was to bung everything into the sections in alphabetical order, and leave someone else to disentangle it all later. But I didn't want to do that. I wanted to get to the bottom of what really happened and present it clearly so that others could see it too. So I had worked and reworked the reports, polishing them until they were perfect, twenty gleaming and shining boxes to be registered with the Magister's Office. That was why I hadn't given in to the nagging of Pascal. I had wanted them to be perfect and only now at the last moment was I going to hand them in at the last possible opportunity: this very afternoon.

I couldn't entirely admit it to the others, how much pleasure this work on the case reports had given me. For them this work was something mildly unpleasant to bear to get what they really wanted - either a better job at the end of it or the paycheck. But for me, it was something more.

As I worked it felt as if my brain was switched on and like a mighty machine gurning into life, creaked and hissed and then as the momentum started to rise, set off in an unstoppable array of motion. The work made me wake up. When I knew I was making progress with a piece of work it is as if my sense of myself and all around me fades away and all that I am left with is the intensity of concentration upon this thing, this task, a hot point of iron carving a streak into the supple world. In work, or this work at least, I was caught up into something not of myself, and that is what I needed, what I wanted, to have this ecstasy of pursuit, the intentness, this forever straining after and running, and to never be at rest. To never have to have the slow pacing self-conscious part of my mind catch up and imprison me. To never be stuck, bored, with nothing to do, nothing to say, nothing to think, a vast dark emptiness like a skyless desert to make me alone.

As it was raining I ate lunch with the others in the break room. Pascal was not there. I felt they needed to know about what happened at the swimming pool, so I told them. Natalie frowned.
'I'm not saying you did the wrong thing,' she said.
'Though it's a little bit too far,' said Caroline.
'But what I am saying,' said Natalie, 'is that whatever you saw, I've heard wonders about that thing. His ex Amie says he gave her the best she ever had - back when they were together in first year.'
'I didn't know he had an ex called Amy,' Caroline said.
'It's Amie with an I and an E,' Natalie said.
'Why did she get rid of him then, if she liked him down there?' I asked.
'She didn't, she was dumped,' said Natalie.
'Oh,' said Caroline. 'Do you think he might have been talking about her, not you, that time in the sandwich shop?'
'What does she look like?' I asked.
'A short girl who looks a little like a pig and who has a tiny whiney voice.'
'He must have been talking about her,' said Caroline.
'Oh,' I said.

I found it hard to concentrate that afternoon. I didn't really do any work and managed to complete an elaborate doodle on a used envelope. Pascal hadn't hated me after all and made fun of me in the shop. Perhaps he had even liked me at the time. But since then I had been cold to him, rude to him, argued with him. I had told him that he was the most disagreeable person I had ever met. And then finally I had publicly humiliated him. I could not imagine him holding anything but abhorrence and contempt for me. Whatever the relationship could have been I had now thrown away. Ruined. It was only now that I realised what I had lost that I...but it didn't matter in any case. I had Barry now.

Feeling guilty I packed up my things and left early. I didn't want to run the risk of seeing Pascal, not after what I now knew.

Wednesday evening
'Another party?' said Barry. 'It's a Wednesday!'
'Why not?' I said. I wore a tight fitting slip dress in white satin and
Barry didn't have anything suitable so I had brought him a clean
white shirt and some chinos.

My uncle's company had hired out St. Leonard's college for their
summer gala. With the students away on their vacation the colleges
did these things. St Leonard's was one of the seafront colleges and
had its own private pier which dated from the Victorian era. The
party was to be held atop the waves.

The glowing pier lights were reflected in the textured sea as we
crossed the quadrangle hand in hand. Inside the music was
swinging and the buffet tables were laden. Waiters scooned around
with trays of drinks.
'This is more of a fancy party,' I said. 'The food is amazing but
you're not allowed to stuff your face. It's against the rules of
poshness.'
'Hey,' said a guy, bouncing into us, 'I can get rid of this loser for
you.'
'Devins!' I said. 'Barry this is my cousin Devins!'
'Scraping the barrel aren't you cuz?'
'Don't be so rude,' I said.
'I'm sorry, I'll get us some more drinks,' Barry said, leaving.
'You're incorrigible,' I said.
'I'm funny,' he said. 'Everyone knows it.'
'You're kidding yourself you deluded oaf,' I said.
'Uh-oh,' he said. 'Looks like we've got a runner.'

I thought Barry had gone to get us some more drinks but I saw him
stumbling rapidly out of the doors, hurrying along the private beach
northwards. I made my excuses and followed him, calling out after
him, but he took no notice. He moved quickly, following the curve
of the coast as the ground rose and I followed as fast as I could. He
climbed right to the top, to where the great mass of the lighthouse
stood, looking beyond the cliffs out at the sea below and the long

deadly drop. I drew near, the wind pulling at my dress. His face was
white and sharp.
'Come down.'
'I'm going to jump.'
'Why?'
'I can't take it anymore.'
'What happened?'
'I just can't stop hating myself. When that guy was talking I felt like
such a failure, such a loser. I can't make anything go right. I can't
make my research to work. I'm such a screw up.'
'You're taking it all too seriously, judging yourself to harshly you-'
'No, you don't understand how important my work is! And I'm
getting to the point where I can't stop it falling apart any more. Life
has become this terrible pressure tearing me apart and I've just had
enough of this feeling. I want it to stop. I want to get out of this life
I've built for myself where I'm constantly being gouged. I want out.
This will make the way the world feels stop.'
'But is it-'
'I've had enough.'
'Why is it so important Barry? Why can't you just rejig your
research, make things easier on yourself?'
'If I give up...I'll have to admit that there is no path to the other
world. I'll have to finally say that it was all a fantasy, that it is only a
TV show not the reality that undergirds existence. I'll have to
accept that there was nowhere for Enid to travel except the land of
death.'

I didn't know what to say. I didn't know what he wanted from him,
what would make him come down. It was melodramatic and a little
ridiculous. Did he want a pity party? I definitely wasn't going to
give him one. That wouldn't help. He needed change.

'And to admit all that would mean the world is too sad to bear. Not
only is my friend dead but everything I believed in is a lie. To admit
all that...the world would be a cold and empty place. There isn't
anything here to protect us from the jagged edges of life. The thing
is I think I have come to that point and I don't want to be part of a

world empty of meaning where every interaction is painful because
everyone is trying to master you. What I want is for the world to
stop. Just stop somehow. To freeze. To give me time to breathe, to
recover from its assaults. But that isn't possible. So I'll have to
leave.'

I stared at him numbly. This was meant to be the bit where I said
something, but what really was there to say? What could get
through to someone whose mind was so messed up.

'Aren't you going to persuade me to stay?'
'Is that what you want? Sympathy? A declaration of love? Someone
to make you feel loved and worthwhile? An elegy to the wonders of
living and the wonders of the world? Some kind of poem?'
'I don't know what I want.'
'Let me tell you what's happening to you. It's called growing up. At
some point we have to realise that we won't get to have our
dreams. We can no longer maintain the fantasies that sustained us
for so long. We have to leave behind some beliefs that we now
know do not fit the world. It's a difficult transition. Our youthful
self judges us and we feel guilty for betraying their hopes. But they
were hopes built on moondust.'
'What did you give up?'
'What?'
'You say it like you've done it yourself. What did you have to give
up?'
'The Prince.'
'What do you mean?'
'I have to stop believing in fairy-tale endings. I used to think that I
would find my prince and walk off into the sunset with him. But I
tried, or rather I'm trying to shrug it all off. Because it isn't real, and
it's so use pretending it is.'
'What is real then?'
'You'll never be able to find out if you're dead.'
'But what if I can't ever find it - true reality?'
'Is that a reason not to try?'
'And Enid?'

'She's gone Barry.'

He started crying, proper crying, howling and blubbering actual hot tears that dropped and dropped. I didn't know anyone had that much water in their face as it kept on coming, loudly wailing, his whole body shaking and flailing. It seemed a long time before the sob quieted into little whimpers of noise and he came down to be closer to me.

Thursday morning
I kept watch over him that night.

That morning we walked from my house over the river and saltmarshes to the physics department on the top of the hill. I waited outside, sitting on the low wall in the sunshine as Barry went inside to meet his supervisor.

As I sat and watched the clouds move across the sky, I wondered if Barry would have the guts to do it, and actually switch track. Or if he would hold back at the last moment and remain stuck in the mud of inaction. And what would I do if he wouldn't change? I couldn't stay and appease him and encourage him in these self destructive choices. I would have to leave him. But how could I do that? It would look heartless to dump someone who has tried to kill themselves. But at the same time I couldn't continue as if nothing had happened.

'It's all sorted,' Barry said, exiting the building. 'We've met together, me and my supervisor, and agreed together that my research will change track and focus on the theoretical rather than the practical. I won't be trying to make a Reality Alteration Device any more.'
'How do you feel?'
'Relieved. Like a huge weight has been taken from me.'
'Come on,' I said. 'I'm taking you to the beach like I promised. Last night wasn't exactly what I had in mind.'

We followed the footpath down to the creek and paid the ferry
fare, and were rowed across to the Shingle Spit, the isolated tongue
on shingle that was separated from the town by the river Blyth and
sat to the north. Here the town rose behind us but felt far away.
We sat down at the top of a shingle rise, looking at the docile waves
that ever rolled in. We sat for a while in silence.

'It doesn't feel like I've given up on Enid and her world,' he said
eventually. 'I think that I stopped believing a long time ago, but I
couldn't admit it to myself. All that suppressed grief didn't do me
any good. But to come now and face up to it all...it wasn't as bad as
I thought.'
'You've already been through the worst of it,' I said.
'Maybe, but I'm still a bit broken. It will be a while before I'm back
on track again.'
'You shouldn't rush these things,' I said.
'Where does that leave you?'
'What do you mean?'
'I'm not exactly the Prince you were waiting for, am I? I mean, look
at me, I'm a mess.'
'Haha, it could be that I was the Prince all along. I mean, I did save
you, didn't I?'
'I don't want you to be my Prince,' said Barry. 'I don't want for you
to forever be rescuing me from myself. I want to learn to be a
different sort of person without you supplying it.'
'Are you dumping me?'
Barry says 'I don't think we can do this. I need to concentrate upon
getting better. Sorting out my life on new terms.'
'I can't believe it but you're right,' I said, relieved.

I didn't want to have a mental boyfriend. Sure, he was a sweet guy
with an even sweeter butt, and I did like him, but it was too much
for me to always be wondering if he were going to go crazy and try
to kill himself again. I didn't want that in my life. And it wouldn't
be good for him either, to know that he could always rely on me to
pull him up, to save him. I didn't want to have to be waiting around
to catch him when he fell, because then he would probably let

himself fall, because my arms are lovely and shapely to fall into. It had to stop, and I was glad that I wasn't the one to do it. Maybe, one day, when all this was over, far in the future, perhaps in another world, we would join together and find we were made for each other. But not here and now.

'Yes,' I said. 'I can't be your nursemaid. You've got to learn to stand on your own feet and face the world. Now is not the time to lean on someone else, use someone else as your defence against life. You've got to just go or it and suck the marrow out of life.'
'There is marrow?'
'The world is a big and wondrous place full of the luminous beauty of things. You've turned your back on it this whole time, rejected it for some reason.'
'I guess I thought it rejected me, so I wanted to insulate myself from it.'
'Rejection is a funny thing,' I said, and my mind flicked to Pascal.

Gulls croaked overhead as we took in the immensity of the sea. The sun hid its face behind a cloud, a gust of wind blew and I shivered momentarily. The tang of salt hit the back of my throat anew.

'Do you know what I think?'
'Your mind is a mystery to me,' I said.
'I think that perhaps it isn't wrong to hope for a Prince. Like me, maybe it isn't wrong to long for some sort of deeper reality. It's just that, as with me, you were looking in all the wrong places. But what if the desire is true? Maybe there really is a Prince who travels to a far country to fight for you and win your heart. Maybe there is some greater truth that we can wake up into, so that our previous life seems like a dream. Maybe there is a hidden tide that flows beneath us?'
'Perhaps, who can say,' I said. 'Whatever it is, it would not be right to expect so high on boyfriends. The relationship can't take the weight, there's no way that they can meet those hopes for the perfect Prince.'

'That sounds sensible.'
'Although I'm not swearing off boys, y'understand.'
'I don't think anyone's asking you to.'
'Do you think I could have a picture of your-'
'No.'
'I had to ask.'

We remained by the sea for the rest of the morning in sun and shade, talking of our hopes for the future, dreaming what we could build.

Thursday afternoon

As I had not slept much last night the majority of the day passed in an exhausted daze. Until Caroline passed by:
'The Director wants to see you,' she said.
'I'm sorry,' I replied. 'I must have heard wrong. I thought you said the Director wanted to see me.'
'Yes that's it,' she said. 'Before the end of the day.'

It was unheard of for an intern to have a one to one meeting with the Director of the Centre. I must have done something incredibly noteworthy. I combed through my memories, trying to think of a particularly good piece of work. Then it hit me. The case reports. I had not filed them. I had meant to, but with everything else going on it had slipped from the top of my mind, what with falling for, rescuing and then breaking up with one boy in a week; whilst at the same time earning the eternal and implacable enmity of another boy.

The case reports were important, if, in Dunwich's obscure and unique code, if they were not filed in time with the Magistrate Judge's office, then the entire case would be deemed void. And there had been twenty that I was meant to file. With an ever deepening lurch in my stomach I realised the awfulness of what I had done, or rather had failed to do. It was a serious enough business for the Centre itself to survive beyond this, but as for my place here, it would be gone. The Director would kick me out immediately. All my dreams for working here, for advancing and finding truth would all be snarled up and shattered. It was over for me. There was no point deferring the inevitable, so trying hard not to cry, I trod the two flights of stairs up to the Director's office.

'Sit down,' said the clipped Director from behind his desk. 'Thank you for coming to see me. You know the importance of these case reports,' said the Director.
'Yes,' I said.
'You can therefore imagine the message I received from the Magister today.'
'I can explain-' I began, even though I couldn't.
'Hush, 'he said. 'It is not often that I have experienced work of this quality.' I didn't say anything at this point, staring at the floor grimly. 'But I should perhaps have expected nothing less than from one of the Wu's...I was with your uncle at college, you know. Before his airline and the chemicals business and the rest of his empire. I always thought he was a genius. Now it turns out that it is a family trait.'
'Sorry?' I said.
'Those case reports you have written for us are works of incredible clarity and insight. You outline the evidence in an extremely helpful manner and all of them will be a great asset to our cause. I can see a great future for you here, and in the field. I will go so far as to offer you a junior position to start next year.'
'That's amazing,' I said, flushed with confusion, relief and delight. Because the case reports had been good. 'But the deposit...they were all filed correctly.'
'Certainly,' he said. 'And on top of everything else I see you have even mastered the art of management and delegation. The reports were filed by a certain P.L. Oyebanjo. Very well done.'

As the door closed behind me I was stunned. Pascal had filed the reports for me. But why? After the way that I had treated him. What could possibly cause him to save me by filing the reports for me. Unless...unless he liked me. No, that wasn't strong enough. Saving someone who had been so hostile to him...could it be, that despite it all, he loved me?

At the end of work that day I found him and called him and we walked silently through the streets until we had reached a part of the beach where it was quiet enough to talk. We sat on the sea wall. 'Thank you,' I said. 'Thank you for filing the reports. If you hadn't then right now I would be history.
'I did say all those times.'
'I know. That annoyed me so much.'
'You've had a lot on your plate and I wanted to help by reminding you.'
'And when I didn't do it.'
'I took it on myself to do it. I didn't want to have to see you leave.'
'But even after arguing with you at every opportunity and insulting you and publicly humiliating you?'
'Amy, I care for you. And if you don't feel the same way, I can understand. But I want to hear it from your lips. Will you have me?'

No one had ever done anything like that for me before. My whole hopes for the future had been saved by an act of love towards me, me who had given nothing to him but contempt. If he had felt anger towards me it must have melted away because now I could see that he kept a corner of his heart warm for me, that I had a place there. How could he show such love to somebody who only gave him trouble? What could it be? Could it be that he found me lovely, that I was lovely? This devotion called out to something in me. Here, finally, someone had gone into battle on my behalf and won my future for me. And, to be fair, before eavesdropping on him I had found him hot. Now there was something entirely princely about him. His love had made me lovely.

'We can give it a try,' I said.
'So long as I'm not your rebound guy.'

'Oh, with Barry. I'm not sure things would have ever worked out with him. But you can wait a bit if you want to be sure I really want you.'
'No I don't want to wait any longer,' he said.
'Yes,' I said, looking deeply into his eyes.
'Only,' he added. 'I have to say. If you want to get me naked there are other ways…'
'I'll try to remember that,' I said.

We kissed there, and then as the sun set we walked off together, holding hands.

PASCAL'S INVESTIGATION

Izzy missing

Izzy's college rang. They suspected that she was missing.
'Suspected?' I said. 'Either she is missing or she isn't.'

Izzy, our beloved daughter, engaged in further studies in Dunwich.
Izzy, our little shy, geeky mascot. Izzy, our precious only child.
Izzy, gone.

'Amy,' I said that night. 'Our daughter is missing.'
'I'm sure she'll turn up,' said my wife.
'This is not an odd sock, it's our daughter. This is serious.'
'She must have been having too much fun, that's all. Don't you
remember being that age, free spirited?'
'That doesn't sound like her. She's hardly what I would call
flamboyant.'
'She is absent minded,' said Amy. 'Look I investigate these sorts of
things all the time. Normally everything is fine.'
'Normally.'
'Look Pascal, don't worry. If we don't hear from her soon I will
make sure that she is found. After all, I have the full weight of the
resources of the Centre behind me. We're the best in the world at
solving mysteries.'
'But why not now?'
'Because it's not fair on her, that's why,' Amy said. 'To go
overboard when she's probably just had a last minute weekend
away. She won't appreciate the trigger friendly intervention, I tell
you.'
'But-'
'Look, in all of our twenty-five years together, when have I failed to
uncover a mystery and get at the truth?'
'That isn't the point and you know it. I want action now!'
'I've got a lot of work to catch up on, find someone else to be
neurotic at,' she said.
'I don't appreciate the-'
But she was gone.

I rang the police. It took a long time to get through to anyone who
knew anything at all. And even then they were not very helpful.
'We find that students usually turn up after a day or two,' said the
sergeant. 'When they come off from their bender.'
'Izzy was not the sort to go on a bender,' I said.
'Mayhaps not, she said. 'But there's been some guy or convention
or research seminar in Oxford and they never thought to tell you.
Just shows how much they think of you, eh?'
'Are you saying that you will not investigate, that you will not
simply pour out your resources unstintingly to find my daughter?'
'No point,' he said. 'Wait another couple of days, see what happens.
We usually see that it was all a false alarm.'
'But it might be too late then.'
'Can't help,' she said.
'I will be writing to our MP about this attitude.'
'Write away,' she said.

I found it incredible and shocking that although my daughter might
be missing and in danger there seemed to be no action at all. Not
from the college. Not from my wife who was now Director of the
Centre for Criminology. Not from the police. She could be in
danger. Time could be critical. What if Izzy couldn't afford to wait
for half a week?

There was nothing else for it. I would have to take the full weight
of the investigation upon myself. I would have to find out the
hazards and dangers which Izzy faced. I would have to be the one
who made a full and detailed investigation and missing person
search. I would be the one who found her.

I made a short list of how to approach the investigation, of facts
that needed to be found. First up, an interview of her College
Tutor, Mrs Godfield, to ascertain the most up to date facts about
her university life - her movements and contacts and likely frame of
mind. With such information to hand I could move quickly and
follow the breadcrumbs of evidence.

I would be a hero when all this was over and she was found.

Mrs Godfield
The next day I left home in Yoxford as usual, getting the diesel train the short distance to Dunwich. But rather than embarking at Holly Hills, in the west of the city, on my daily commute, I continued on to Dunwich central station. I had taken off a few days from my job as Events Manager for a large corporation which was based in Dunwich for legal reasons. I wanted to make a thorough investigation about what had happened to Izzy. Arriving at the station I walked the remainder of the way up to Izzy's College. Up past the red brick Cathedral and the ornate frontage of the Eastern Shires Regional Assembly. Further past the Garrison onto where Hook Green opened out to my right. There Dunwich Lido still stood beside the river, where Amy showed how desperate she had been to get my kit off. Time and long marriage had obviously eroded that first enthusiasm for each other. It's the same for everyone. Still further walking onwards, over the causeway and the salt marshes, then the bridge over the River Dunwich, before the gentle rise of the hill, up to St. James' Corner and then the Hill Campus, where Cromwell College, among others, stood.

As I made the walk I worried about Izzy. She was still so young, so defenceless. There was so much that she didn't understand about the world. She had hardly been perceptive, devoted as she was to her interests, whatever they were. She would have been an easy person to take advantage of.

Izzy's tutor, Mrs Godfield, met me in the lobby of Cromwell College, before taking me to an empty room which I presumed was used for counselling. She offered me some refreshments, which I declined, wanting to get to business as quickly as possible.
'We have not met before,' she said. 'But I am Izzy's tutor.'
'What can you tell me?' I asked.

'She has not attended any of her appointments or eaten in the dinner hall or picked up any of her post for three days now. The police have been informed that it is possible that she is missing, but it is still too early to make an official investigation. She might have simply taken off out of town.'

'Shouldn't you be investigating as soon as possible?'

'Although it is not technically allowed within our bylaws during term-time to leave the city, the truth is that students often leave the city for conferences and festivals and mini-breaks and funerals and camping trips and temporary work and many other things. The inconsiderate mites simply don't think to let us know half the time. If we were to follow up with a criminal investigation every extended absence we would be accused of grossly wasting police time. It is simply not feasible.'

'I will have to do my best to find what I can when the trail is still fresh.'

'If you have the resources I would recommend the investigations unit of the Centre for Criminology. Very discrete and reassuringly expensive.'

'No, I'll do it myself,' I said. 'What can you tell me about what Izzy was doing? Her friends? Her interactions? Her research?'

She clicked her tongue and sighed.

'The thing you must understand Mr Oyebanjo, is that in my role of College Tutor, it is more of a role of administrative oversight. I am responsible for her official records, which in the eyes of the university is an almost sacred role. It contains all that is needful to know about her, from the university's point of view. Unfortunately in this case the university found Isabel relatively uninteresting and the record is largely blank.'

'The prospectus says that pastoral care is vested in the College Tutor.'

'Whilst that is undoubtedly true, we had no reason to believe there were any pastoral concerns.'

'But now she is missing.'

'You must understand Mr Oyebanjo, that I know almost nothing about her personally. I cannot even recall if I have even met Isabel.

But in any case, I would imagine that her own father would know more about her friends, activities and research progress than a mere college functionary. You see?'

'I think my wife might know some things. The female bond.'

'Quite. I suggest that you ask her in that case.'

'And failing that?'

'If you wish further information you should contact her academic supervisor, Dr Barry Hincliffe. He would have been in daily contact with her and she would have been based in his department. He would be intimately aware of her research and have had a great deal of face to face contact with her. If you wish for a more personalised and up-to-date report on her mindset, I advise you apply to Dr. Hincliffe. I will even arrange an appointment for you with him tomorrow if you like.'

'Yes that would be helpful,' I said.

'If you wait for several minutes I will confirm this for you.'

As I had most of the day remaining I went to walk along the seafront. In the winter chill many of the seaside shops had closed for the season, their shutters closed. I leant on the railings and looked out to the sea. The tide was out and distant. I thought about Izzy. Where was she? Was she alive? Was she dead? Was she this very moment crying out for help from somewhere. Through my mind flashed every worst case scenario. But something told me that she no longer walked the earth. If there was an innocent explanation then we could have expected some inkling of this sort of behaviour from her before. But it was so out of character. Which suggested that this dramatic absence did not come from her but from someone else. Someone had caused her to go away. And I could not believe that this someone had her best interests at heart. It was vital that I find her before it was too late. But what if it was too late? What if she was dead?

Memory
I remember.

When she was three Izzy had a severe illness. We spent much time at the hospital. From the hospital window beside her bed I could see the sea. In those days the sea had its own moods which turned and slid. Now bright, then disfigured, soon cold and clear. Next clouded with impenetrable fogs, then ruffled and riled with cold blasting wind. All the city gathered around its shores, and it remained their constant companion. Its chills, storms and disquiets ruled us. The sea's moods mirrored the moods of the girl: capricious, both implacable and quick. She was not getting better.

Holding her there I felt as if I would never again be so close to another breathing body. The air flowing through our nostrils is the same. I would never be so close to another person.

In that ward I realised that this action of begetting a child will live on further than anything else I do. Yet fathers are always losing their children. If not in the first few years like this hospital agony then they must wait until time itself wrenches the little ones from their grasp, as these dependent warm small clinging hands grow larger and no longer reach out. If I did not lose little Isabel now I would have had to surrender her later - to an unknown woman, shadowy and distant. She would be swallowed up into a woman, a woman who I would barely know. A woman whose mind and heart would be hidden to me. In the early years I was Isabel's entire world, whole and perfect. But later, who can say. I imagined myself an old man, desperate for any ray of light to shine from the glance of the now grown Isabel's face, and it would be too fleeting, too distant, too pitying. I would altogether be too much in darkness. No, much better that I should keep Isabel forever mine like this. What perfect, piercing sadness; to hold forever in my heart a child who gave me the fullness of her love. Those small hands, holding around his neck, cupping as if existence itself depended upon it, both delicate and tight.

In those days beyond all else: the rawness, the exhaustion, the frayed edge of grief: a desperate emptiness. The claws of nothingness laid upon his heart and scraping deep. Death, the old enemy, death.

Fortunately she recovered. But those fretful days at the hospital still haunted me. Were they returning now? Are we again grappling with the death of our daughter? Has it already happened?

I told all this to Amy that evening, my reflections and my memories.
'I don't know where you get all that from. Some movie you watched no doubt. Because you were never here when Izzy was young.'
'I was around.'
'You were still doing your poetry tours.'
'I stopped them, took a regular job to be here with all of you.'
'Even then you were hardly here. There was so much you didn't see. So much blood and guts you'll never know. You only waltzed in, kissed them on their drowsy foreheads and closed the door.'
'I kissed them goodnight every single night.'
'But it's not the same as living through the screaming and the tears and every giggling laugh.'
'I was at the hospital when it all happened. When she was three.'
'You did one night shift. I was there for weeks, never leaving her side.'
'I brought you grapes.'
'I ask this time and time again Pascal. Why don't you see things as they are? What is it about your mind that is bent upon invention?'
'You're impossible.'
'You never were very good at seeing reality for what it is. You're fantasising.'
'Sometimes I wish-'
'Think what you want then. Fool yourself if you wish. But know that I am not deceived.'

The conviction grows within me. She is dead. With every passing day, every passing hour, it becomes a more likely conclusion to this affair. If I cannot find her alive I will find who is responsible for her death and I will make them pay. I don't know what it is that makes me so sure that something terrible has happened to her. But it is a horrifying, almost certain, conviction. Call it a father's intuition if you will.

It is the meeting with Izzy's supervisor tomorrow. This Dr Hincliffe must know something. But why hasn't he come forward with information? There's something a little suspect going on, but I won't know what it is until the meeting tomorrow.

Now that she is no longer here, the memories of Izzy's childhood are now oppressive to me. Mocking.

Barry Hincliffe

The next day I set out to interview the witness. Dr Hincliffe's office was in the physics department at the top of the hill campus. It had been a long time since I had anything to do with the university and the sight and smell of the lecture halls reminded me of my own younger days. Of the time I had met Amy. She was different now.

'Ah Pascal,' said Hincliffe. His office was narrow and lined with books and untidy papers. There was barely room for me to sit. 'Come in.' I had the sense that I had met him before but could not remember. 'You look just the same. Sit down.'
'Indeed,' I said.
'I can guess why you're here. Your daughter. Izzy.'
'Yes.'
'As far as I'm aware I'm the last person to see her.'
'And why was that?'
'Who can say for sure? Only her, and now she's gone and disappeared on us. Goodness me!'
'Tell me what happened.'
'Naturally. She was having dinner here with my wife and I. We do that for my graduate students. After eating we talked, as we often do of life and work and our interests. But this night she sounded different:

"I can feel the call stronger than ever," she said. I enquired what manner of call this might be. "It is a sort of pull," she explained. "As if I am being hurled through a magnetic field. As if something out there is drawing me. Like an itch that I can't shake. I know that over there I have to go."
"But why?"
"I have never felt at home here."
"In Dunwich?"
"No, in this world. And now I am being called."
"I don't know about that," I said. "I don't know if it is quite safe. Or even real, what you are trying to do."
"Look at me. Look into my eyes. I am serious. Do you really think that this world is made of what we can see or touch? That there isn't a hidden tide rolling beneath us? The true nature of things pokes out here and there like spring grass through snow. That it is the most important thing, to stand upon the dust of this other, hidden, transcendent world and breathe its air. Would you deny me that?"
"Very well," I said, half-wearily and half filled with a humbling awe at her faith. And she walked from me, vanishing into the shadows.'

'I see,' I said. I wasn't sure what Hincliffe was implying here. 'It sounds very suspect. But can you be any more specific?'
'The thing that was difficult - is difficult - about all this for me is that she was trying to do in her research what I had failed to do. What I had even given up trying to do many years ago. To construct a RAD. A Reality Alteration Device. Based upon a complex mathematical model of interlocking realities it intends to collapse...but I see that I am losing you in the technicalities. Izzy was attempting to do something that no one had ever done before. It had stretched her to the very edge, beyond it even, the impact of such an effort was very sore indeed. There was no way for me to help her there. In fact I had thought that she would fail and her whole PhD would implode. But that night she whispered that she had built a prototype and would try it out. I was sceptical, of course

I was. But now she has disappeared I understand that she must have found a way to make it work.'
'What exactly do you think has happened to her?'
'Did you ever feel as if you were waiting for your life to start? As if this whole time you had been dreaming?'
'No.'
'That will make it harder to explain,' said Hincliffe. 'Let's put it like this. There are lots of people who think they know Izzy. After all, there is plenty about her which is striking: her enormous intelligence, her strong self belief, her undeniable beauty, her struggles with mental illness. But there is another side to Izzy which few see immediately. Working with her closely in the Physics Department I saw an aspect of her life and character which she guarded closely. I am talking about her devotion to the classic 80s sci-fi show Hoshi-Henro, an obsession which we both shared. I remember her telling me her love story with the stars which led her both into physics and science fiction,' he said. 'And I was captivated by it. It was something which led us into friendship together. She would come here and we would watch episodes and argue obsessively over the minutiae of the HH universe such as-'
'I am not here to listen to trivia.'
'Very well. Let me see now...what else...Her progress through her PhD was not smooth. It was a difficult subject and the mathematics involved surpassed the abilities of the majority of the faculty....however, despite all this, she made the final breakthrough. She was called onwards, activated the RAD, and was transferred...into the stars and who knows, maybe to the Hoshi-Henro starship itself.'
'Is that your idea of a joke?'
'Not at all, I'm perfectly serious. Although it shakes me to the core the most likely explanation is that Izzy has been subsumed and swallowed up into the world of Hoshi-Henro where she truly belongs.'
'You are crazy.'
'You wouldn't be the first to call me that. I had even lost faith for many years that such a move was possible...but now...you see there was a girl I knew many years ago and she vanished too and I

persuaded myself she must be dead, but do you see, she never died either. They both transferred to a greater reality!'

As I left the college I was left with the unshakable conclusion that he must have killed her. No one could be that crazy. It must be a ludicrous cover for what he has done. He murdered my daughter.

The Body
It was not long after I arrived back home that day that the telephone rang. It was Mrs Godfield again. I was surprised to hear her after only speaking yesterday.
'There are a few things that I now need to disclose to you, now that a new stage has been reached,' she said.
'What new stage?'
'Hadn't you heard? A body was found washed up this morning from the sea.'
'Izzy?'
'Apparently the damage to the ahem...it is not possible for a visual identification and so must be sent for a professional assessment in Ipswich. It may take several days.'
'Thank you for updating me as the case progresses.'
'That wasn't the information I wanted to disclose,' she said. 'Isabel had been struggling with her mental health for some time. She had indeed been referred to a special practitioner because of her self harming. We had thought that she had been making great strides, that these incidents lay firmly in the past but...'
'Why was I not told of this.'
'It is confidential medical records,' she said. 'It can't be shared. Except now the investigative team are considering suicide among the possibilities, we decided on compassionate grounds to inform you.'
'Let me know any new information,' I said, and put the phone down.

I wasn't concerned about the suicide warning. The body confirmed my suspicions. I already was sure what had happened. Barry

Hincliffe had killed her. It was not hard to reconstruct events. The loopy academic who already had a loose grip on reality, drew close to Izzy the student he was supervising. Perhaps he fell in love with her. One day he confessed his feelings and she rejected him. In a rage he attacked her and she died. Perhaps he hadn't intended to kill her, but it had happened. Then he disposed of the body at sea on a stormy night. Only the body had returned to cause him trouble.

Unless of course it was different. Izzy and Hincliffe could have been having a clandestine romantic relationship for some time. It was not unknown for a teacher and student to develop reciprocal feelings for each other, even though it is a gross violation of power and responsibility. So let's say they had this relationship as they shared so much in their lives, had in common the physics and that show they liked and a certain awkwardness too. But then they argued. There would be arguments. She would want to make their relationship public, she wasn't ashamed of their connection. He wanted to keep it hidden, fearing for his job. So they argued, and entirely accidentally things got out of hand, and he hadn't meant to hurt her, but he was too clumsy and she had been hit by something and at first he didn't realise how badly she was hurt and then he desperately tried to revive her and gradually and limply sunk into despair as he saw that she was gone. He dumped the body at sea. But in his heart he knew that it was not over, and that she would always hang over him. Yes. That is entirely persuasive. This is the version that my investigation is supporting.

'Her body has been found,' I said to Amy that evening. She was doing the washing up and I was sitting with the index cards of evidence that I had been putting together.
'No it hasn't. A body has been found. It happens about once a month because of the smugglers.'
'Won't you at least admit she is missing.'
'She is missing, but the best thing to do is to let the official agencies handle it.'
'I can't leave my precious daughter in their hands.'

'You never showed that much interest in her before. You were always more interested in the latest celebrity book signing.'
'I have always been involved with her life Amy. I don't know how you can say such things.'
'Then tell me one thing about the TV show that she loved so much and was her passion and her life. If you were as involved as you say you are, you would have entered into her interests.'
'It was called Honi-Hesho and-'
'Exactly.'
'Never mind that. I have to tell you about Barry Hincliffe. I went to see him today.'
'You really shouldn't have.'
'I did. And he's a really creepy guy. He took her around to his house and they spent whole evenings there together. Predatory, that's what I'd call it.'
'We've heard that story before. It's ugly and tired. The world doesn't need to hear another iteration.'
'All that matters is what's true. I thought you of all people would be able to appreciate that,' I said.
'But that's just what I'm saying. Barry's not got it in him. He's harmless. He's married now. Has two kids. Perfectly regular guy, for a Dunwich academic.'
'You can never know what somebody is capable of given the opportunity.'
'Come on, you knew him, back in the day. He tagged along with the gang sometimes. You know, Natalie and Caroline and Peter.'

I wrinkled my head in concentration.
'That shifty skeletal guy who used to stare at your tits? There's something wrong with him,' I said. 'Always was.'
'Don't have a go at Barry, alright. And I don't want to hear any more of your hysterical theories.'
'I will find out his darkest secrets, anything to find out what happened to my girl.'
'I'll give you a head start. I shagged him once.'
'What? When?'
'Back when we were interns. And it-'

'This proves my point. He is a corrupter of young women.'
'No silly. I had to seduce him, he was so clueless. He wouldn't know where to start.'
'You'll see that I am right.'
'Whatever. At least try to find out a bit about Hoshi-Henro. The least you could do is to connect with your real daughter, not the fantasy one you constructed as soon as the inconvenient reality clocked out for a couple of days.'

The Hoshi-Henro Encyclopaedia
That night I flicked through Izzy's worn book looking at entries. The Hoshi-Henro encyclopaedia.

> Season 1 Episode 1: Exodus. Due to environmental catastrophe - the atmosphere was boiling off the earth - the planet was abandoned. For humanity to survive, a great migration of spaceships was launched in the search for a new home planet.

> Octavin - the powerful energy source which powers intergalactic life and travel.

> Spacewhale - Spacewhale, the Cetasta,

> Hoshi-Henro - A turtle shaped hunting ship, class C, fitted with eight small ships for hunts. The crew continually fail to catch the spacewhales required for the functioning of the human fleet.

> Tiumi - shape shifting aliens.

> Tubcleaner - a strong alcoholic beverage distilled by Itsuki, ostensibly for medicinal use. It has been known to spread into the wider space economy and has gained a reputation. The recipe is to ferment grain with sugar cane, before distilling in batches.

Enid (Capt.) - is the Captain of the Hoshi-Henro. Brave and resolute she is the figure that inspires the entire ship, the beating heart of the Hoshi-Henro, and her charisma is undeniable. While she sometimes leaps before she looks, with the help of her crew gathered around her she pulls through any situation and faces down the deadliest foes. Small in stature but big on determination and grit, she is known equally by her skill with the spacelance and her faultless intuition. Her courage has never failed.

Huro (Aux. Comm.) - is the second in command aboard the ship, and Hunt Chief. He is strong in body and mind, and his physical and mental toughness has won the day many times. He typically carries with him a lance of great weight and size. A man of few words, he cares deeply about those who are important in his life. Whilst known to attack first and ask questions later, his devotion to Captain Enid is absolute and unflinching. He reigns black blood and death upon the ship's enemies.

Dr. Itsuki (Aux. Comm.) - is the ship's doctor and a decorated war hero. His lower body was blown off in the explosion at Arubama (Season 1 Episode 6) and now uses a *pedmimator* to move, and a number of other mechanical assistances for his other needs. In personality he is positive, encouraging, empathetic and popular, and his sunny disposition has often given the crew the hope they need in tough times. His brown bearded face and open grin are complemented by the bulging muscles of his upper body. Itsuki's medical knowledge and skill has saved many lives aboard the Hoshi-Henro.

Baleine (Sec. Dir.) - is the ship's Navigation Director. Full of energy, she thrives in the stimulation of sharing ideas and is a member of the Academy of Scholars. Decisive, insightful and efficient, Baleine enjoys a challenge, and delights in achieving the ship's goals. Quick talking, engaging and impatient, her mouth can sometimes get her into trouble. This is perhaps the origin of her rivalry with Officer Reiji. With generous curves and flaming red hair, Baleine is not afraid to challenge others where necessary to bring the crew to new understandings.

Dr. Eiko (Off.) - Is the ship's Science Officer. Careful and questioning, inventive and creative, her focus is upon rolling back the fogs of ignorance. She has a thirst for knowledge which means that she is open minded and constantly assessing ideas. In her personal relationships she is a very private person and can appear shy. Short and slight in stature, she can often be seen working late at night in her lab on her latest personal research project. Above all else the brilliance of her intellect has saved the Hoshi-Henro many times.

Pequod (Off.) - is the ship's Security Officer. Immersed in strategic thought he presents plans and a systematic perspective on the problems the Hoshi-Henro faces. Independent, hard working, analytical and socially gauche, Pequod can be equally intense and disengaged in relation to those around him. Tall, slim and dark, Pequod is highly committed to the life of the mind, and this can leave him to neglect other considerations. He is an aficionado of the game Vero.

Reiji (Off.) - is the ship's Technical Officer. Risk loving and fun she adores all things machines. She can often be seen relaxing with a drink and sharing an earthy joke at the end of the working day, and brings a sense of life and energy wherever she goes. Bold, practical, sociable and defiant she loves getting dirty and figuring things out. Tall and with a penchant for flirtatiousness, Reiji will always take a bet and never turn down a dare. Most of all, the ship itself, the Hoshi-Henro, has never been so cared for as under the hands of Reiji.

Tiring I flipped to the episode outline of the final episode.
    Season 5 Episode 10: Home. After the revelation that the Spacewhales hold the key to a new home planet, and the defeat of the Space-Whaling Corporation, the Hoshi-Henro leads the journey in which the whales are followed not hunted. They arrive at their new home planet, living in harmony with the creatures of the universe.

I let the book close once more. Enid, Huro, Itsuki, Eiko, Reiji. These were the people more real to Izzy than me. It was distasteful that somehow the minutiae of a second-rate sci-fi show had somehow become more real to her than her blood and flesh father. According to Hincliffe she had left us to be part of that world. Perhaps that's what he liked to tell himself, that it was her version of heaven after he had killed her. I wondered what sort of expression had been on Izzy's face as the mild mannered professor turned and killed her, what he put her through. I would trap him and prove him guilty of this terrible crime against my daughter. Already my investigations were closing in around him. He had been the last person to see him. He had no alibi. The weight of evidence lay against him. I would destroy him for what he did to Izzy.

Barry Hincliffe Missing
'Barry is now missing,' said Amy the next day. 'His wife reported it.'

It was the afternoon and she had returned from work early, probably to tell me this news. I was still off from work and staying in the house, waiting for and making phone calls. She had made a cup of tea and had sat down in the living room. The birds were singing outside in the garden and the skies were shot through with red through the clouds.

'He's missing?' I said.

'Maybe he ran away after you hounded him. Perhaps something worse.'

'It only makes sense,' I said. 'Having killed Izzy, he now sees that he cannot escape justice, and so he decides to evade capture. He commits suicide.'

'No body has been found.'

'It's only a matter of time, believe me,' I said.

'Two missing people,' she said shaking her head. 'Both of whom knew each other. This is a mystery that will take more than your two minutes of deductions and amateur sleuthing.'

'So you finally admit that Izzy is missing then.'

'Yes,' she said.

'I told you from the start that she was,' I said. 'And in time you'll come to the same inevitable conclusions as me. As will the police. Hincliffe did it.'

'Can you PLEASE stop,' she said. 'Stop this premature slander. And stop having it in for Barry.'

'There's no need to shout.'

She sat back and I could see her attempt to master and control her anger. It's something that she has improved at over the years. I enjoy watching the clenched teeth relax and the heavy breathing subside. It gives me hope that things can be gained over a marriage as well as lost.

'How is it you're so confident that she's ok?' I asked, exasperated.

'Because I know Barry,' she said. 'And because...you wouldn't know this, but because of a conversation I had with her. She was struggling with her studies and was thinking of giving it up. She was self-harming.'

'You knew about that?'

'Izzy came to me,' she said. 'And I told her that it didn't have to be this way, that the whole world lay before her. And she told me not to worry, that she knew that she couldn't slash her wrists, she couldn't bear the blood she had found out. And she wouldn't be able to throw herself from a height. She said that if she were to kill herself she would hire a car and a quiet cottage with a garage and tape all the holes up and leave the engine on and fall asleep forever

to carbon monoxide poisoning. But she said she wasn't going to do
that: that what she wanted to do was not go to sleep but wake up.'
'I don't see how that depressing anecdote gives you confidence.'
'Because it rules things out. That's what we do at the Centre, we
rule things out. We use logic to find out the truth. I know you
worked there for a year, but that barely gives a flavour of the tools
we have at our disposal. Once we eliminate the impossible,
whatever remains, no likely how improbable, must be the truth.
The more that we can eliminate, the clearer the picture we can
have. So that conversation with Izzy has helped a lot.'
'To me it proves a morbid state of mind,' I said.

By this point in the conversation the sun had set and neither of us
had got up to turn on any lights. As darkness reached its hand over
the skies, so darkness too filled our rooms, our home. We sat there
in the shadows, a deep abyss of darkness between us. I could barely
see her face.

'I blame you, you know,' I said.
'Why does that not surprise me,' Amy said. 'How exactly is all this
my fault?'
'It was from you that she got this fanaticism about that TV show.'
'That's giving me far too much credit,' Amy said. 'One rainy bank
holiday weekend she found a stack of the old videos in the garage
and after that there was no stopping her. It really grabbed her. I
didn't do anything, let alone brainwash her.'
'But you liked the show too, didn't you?'
'Millions of people liked the show when it was on. There's nothing
special about that.'
'But you were pleased when she took it up?'
'Don't we always like sharing parts of our lives with our children -
our own interests and childhoods and ideas. It's like living through
the excitement again, seeing it through their eyes, and passing part
of yourself on, a small part of you living into the next generation.
Haven't you shared anything of yourself with her? You must have.'
'Children don't appreciate poetry.'
'That is absolutely not true.'

'Let's not have that argument again. And it's getting better. The point is that it's through you that this dangerous obsession was introduced.'
'Why shouldn't she like Hoshi-Henro? Why shouldn't she have interests and passions?'
'She might well have taken it too far.'
'What do you mean?'
'Her rabid interest in the thing seems to have sparked the interest of Hincliffe and led down this entire troublesome track.'
'Give it up on Barry. Please.'
'I will visit Mrs Hincliffe tomorrow for the final corroboration of my theory, and then I will file my investigation with the police. Thereafter I will not concern myself with it any longer. If he's dead too then there's no more justice that I can find.'
'You're not meant to be doing this you know. It's not right to barge into the home of a distressed person and put suggestive questions to her.'
'You can't stop me. It's not illegal for two people to have a conversation.'

She sighed and left the room, and I saw the orange glow of the stairs light as she made her way upstairs. I would have to prepare for tomorrow. I would have to use everything at my disposal to get Mrs Hincliffe to speak and reveal facts to undeniably support my argument.

Mrs Hincliffe
The Hincliffes' house was in Theberton, a cottage in Suffolk Pink opposite the thatched parish church.

'Mrs Hincliffe? I'm from the agency,' I said.
'Oh do come in, and call me Doreen,' she said. 'There has been ever so much paperwork to fill in I've got ever so flustered with all the groups and agencies.'
'Quite understandable.'

She made me a cup of tea and we sat in the kitchen.

'It's been terrible,' she said. 'I don't know what to think. It's not like him to go off...do you think he might be...'

'The likelihood is that he has passed away,' I said.

'An accident do you think?'

'Or something else. He might have taken his own life. We are still investigating.'

'If I could help in any way?'

'Yes, we require something of a cross-section of his personality to aid our inquiries. How would you describe him?'

'He was a quiet man. Liked his hobbies. He was making a model of that spaceship from that old show out of matchsticks. Never finished. Where did you say you were from again?'

'What about his health?'

'Good enough. He did struggle with his mental health. Depressed for years, but don't mention that at the funeral. If there is to be a funeral. Never quite managed to stay on top. He was always a funny one. Not funny haha funny like strange.'

'What about his students?'

'He seemed to get on fine. Now and then one or two would take to him, and he would bring them back here for a tea on a Sunday afternoon and I would look after them a bit because they never had a clue. Most often after the tea they would settle down on the settee to watch that tv show. He did it recently with that girl, you know, the one they think died. He was very upset when she went missing. Or he was at first. Then he started laughing about it and whispering strange things under his breath like 'after all these years.' It must have driven him off the edge, poor thing.'

'An unusual friendship, between a young woman and an older man?'

'He was unusual, that's the short of it,' she said. 'And got much stranger in the last week. He got dredging up things from the past, of this school friend called Enid that he had, and seemed to think that the same sort of thing was due for this Izzy. And he was saying the wildest things. Things that just can't be true.'

'What sort of things?'

'He said...what was it now... "They *actually - somehow - travelled into space and are now roaming the galaxy past desolate moons and majestic spacewhales. And all I can think of is...I want to join them. Now I feel something within me stir. I will place my own shoes in their footprints and follow, if I am able.*" You don't think it was code for, you know, topping himself?'

'When did you see him last?'

'He said he was going out for a walk that night, the night he disappeared. It was a cold and foggy night and he slipped away into the marsh gloom. But he didn't come back. He said that he wanted to meet those dead girls and I didn't stop him. He must have thrown himself into the marshes, poor thing.'

'It must be hard, but this is very important, I have to ask about his sexual proclivities.'

'All that stopped a long time ago,' she said. 'We've had other things to think about.'

'And you don't think that he ever went anywhere else…?'

'No, not likely. That man had such a tenuous connection to the world I don't think he even noticed women, let alone could organise an affair. He would have been hopeless at it. Whatever else, I know there was nothing like that involved in his disappearance.'

'And your own children?'

'Just the twins - off at university in Bristol. They haven't heard yet about all this. I imagine they'll do alright.'

'You have been very helpful so far...the only thing is that, as you say, he was not proficient when it comes to woman, how it was that the two of you-'

'Chalk and cheese dear, chalk and cheese. Let me tell you how it all happened. I had been his cleaner, believe it or not, when he first started as a lecturer. I hadn't had much to do with him. He had been high and inaccessible, but I believe he liked having me about the place, making it homely, making it liveable and less empty and austere. He was a bit of a cold fish. But one day before I started I was doing the crossword and I couldn't get some of the clues and he couldn't resist and spat out the answers. We started doing the crossword every day then with a cuppa, and then I started to feed

him some proper food. When I went away for the summer, two months later he confessed how much he missed having me around, that the house seemed colder and darker and altogether quieter without me there, and he didn't want to hear the noise of his own brain in the evening. I was cosy and comfortable and fit with his life, and he realised that. As for me, once I got together with him I didn't have to be a cleaner any more. And I always had a little thing for the stuttering shy handsome professor. So all in all, it happened and before we knew it we were married!'
'So not an affair of passion?'
'Barry is not that sort of a person. He is logical and precise.'
'I see.'
'I hope this has been some help to track him down. If you can. If there's still a chance.'
'Thank you for your help. It has been very helpful.'
'I can't bear to think of him out there, dying all alone. He really must have lost his sense of what was what. I should have seen it, I should have.'
'Everyone is alone in the end,' I said. 'Now I must leave.'
'Before you go do you want to see the matchstick model? Go on, see the model. It's what he would have wanted.'

After meeting with Doreen I had to accept the inevitable. Barry could not have killed Izzy. He had always been a pathetic little man incapable of taking the initiative. That had never changed. He would not have ever had the guts to make a move on anyone. His was that type, the natural victim of the world, who always was passive. His was the fear and weakness that opted out of the world. I had to accept that this was what he had done. That it meant that Izzy must herself have made the same choice. Izzy had killed herself.

Amy's gambit
I told Amy the result of my investigation that night.

'It's all about the evidence,' I said. 'At first I thought that Hincliffe had killed Izzy, and then killed himself - either out of horror at his actions, or because he knew I would catch him. But I've come to see that this reconstruction is not plausible, given the people involved. It is much more likely that Izzy killed herself, and then heartbroken, Hincliffe followed suit.'

'Really?' asked Amy, arching an eyebrow.

'But there remains the motivation to settle. Did they think that killing themselves would get them to this other world? That it was the means of transference? They might have clothed it up in fancy technical terms, but that is what they meant. The other option is that they both had become overcome with sadness and despair. I'm not sure which is worse. Both are insane, clearly.'

'There is one option you have not considered,' said Amy.

'What's that?'

'That Izzy and Barry might have been telling the truth.'

'I'm sure they thought they were, that's the worst of it,' I said.

She leaned back in her armchair.

'I received a note from the mortuary in Ipswich today,' she said. 'They've identified the body that washed up. It's not Izzy or Barry. It's a Lithuanian drug mule.'

'That doesn't prove anything.'

'That's what I've been saying all along,' said Amy. 'You've been leaping ahead of the proof. Constructing elaborate fancies.'

'So if Izzy and Barry are still missing and out there somewhere they could be fine, or dead, or dying. They could even be somewhere together. Anything is possible.'

'Exactly.'

'I've still got a terrible feeling that they're dead.'

'There is no evidence to suggest that,' said Amy.

'If they aren't dead, what do you think has happened to them?'

She paused and became uncharacteristically quiet.

'I'm starting to believe,' said Amy eventually, in a whisper.

'Believe what?'

'What Izzy believed. I've been looking through some of her notes and despite myself it's...I can't describe it.'
'I would never have guessed you would be the sort of person to fall for these fairy tales.'
'No, I'm saying it wrong. It isn't so much belief as doubt.'
'Now you are making no sense at all.'
'No. It's doubting that this world is all there is. It can't hold up for me any more. I've come to doubt that what we see with our eyes is the whole picture. That there isn't a whole another level rolling and roaring beneath us. The hidden tide.'
'God, not you as well. I'm surrounded by imbeciles. Come on then. Explain yourself.'

She took a deep breath.
'Doesn't it seem a bit fabricated to you?'
'What?'
'This place. This Dunwich with its lack of electricity, the town that time forgot.'
'No, not at all. Because there is a scientific explanation. It's all down to the electromagnetic radiation from the research centre.'
'Just because there's a scientific explanation doesn't mean that there isn't another complementary explanation.'
'Look the problem is this insistence upon fabrication of a fake world. You surely can't be taken in by that. I know you think the world is good and full of wonder. You don't want to escape the world. Not like Hincliffe. You're too caught up with the joy of living. This world is not purely an illusion.'
'Fabrication is the wrong word. I don't really mean that. You're right, I don't think the world is an illusion. It's just that it refers to something else, that it's incomplete as it is. That what we perceive is not the whole truth, because there is an invisible world. What I'm saying is that it's not about trying to escape from the world but it is to enter an intensification. This world is the shadow, the dim reflection. But the real thing is out there - this world on steroids.'
'But you can't prove it!'
'Of course I can't, and you can't prove it isn't true. Just as if there's no way to say for sure whether you're dreaming from within a

dream and if a world of wakefulness exists somewhere. We can't prove if this world refers only to itself, or if it is the shadow of a greater reality. But I feel those sparks rising. We're filled with longings that this world can't fully satisfy. Perhaps the explanation is that we were made for a different world.'

'I don't know what to say,' I said. 'Are you going to vanish too along with them?'
'I wouldn't even know where to begin,' Amy said. 'And I'm still not sure. There are so many unanswered questions. So many things that still trouble me.'
'So you're not persuaded then?'
'On the key point I am persuaded. That the most logical explanation is that they really have been washed away by the hidden tide into the stars.'
'Surely if we find their bodies this whole edifice of thought will collapse.'
'Yes.'
'Hadn't you better wait then before you make your conclusions?'
'I don't feel that I need to wait.'

The conversation had quickly eluded my control. We were in territory that I never expected to have to navigate. I wondered how to get her in for some sort of assessment.

'Do you understand how crazy what you are saying is?'
'How so?'
'It's silly, there's no other word for it. This is the real world. There is no other. Come back to reality.'
'It's better to be awake than to live in a dream world and sleep away your life.'
'But look here. It's quite ridiculous, that's the truth of the matter. But even if it weren't, even if another world existed it would be impossible for you to leave this supposed dreamworld. How can the atoms of your body be transferred from here into another world, for all we know, trillions of light years away? Just think about it. It's impossible for you to leave.'

'No, not at all. It doesn't work like that. It's just as easy as waking from sleep.'

SPACE SICKNESS PART 1 BY MATT GREENFORD & BARRY HINCLIFFE

Introductory Scene

On screen images of the Horsehead Nebula and the Pleiades and the Hubble Deep Field.

Voiceover: Space. Its immensity is incomprehensible. There are vast tracts of interstellar emptiness. Many billions of galaxies and innumerable galaxy clusters overwhelm us. The incandescent star fields leave us shuddering with their beauty. The gelid wastes of space and the superheated supergiants are extremities our bodies cannot bear. Here there are forces more intense than we can master; here the laws of physics corral us and limit us, mocking our finite span: we could never travel the width of space, or scale its height, or span its depth, for many trillions of light years cover the face of the deep. And then there are the Spacewhales.

Hoshi-Henro comes into view entering a strange nebula.

Voiceover: It is not surprising that the human mind is unable to process such magnitudes, staring into it every day, insulated from it by only a thin metal skin. We travel through it, without sunlight or wind on our cheeks, never knowing if we will be able to lay our heads down and rest. We should have expected the neurology of the brain to react adversely when facing both a challenging present and an uncertain future.

Theme Sequence Plays. A shot of the turtle-shaped Hoshi-Henro passing overhead is shown then a pan of the entire earth fleet before the main crew have their establishing shots; Captain Toxequo; Huro - Hunt Commander; Science Officer Eiko; Security Officer Pequod; Navigator Baleine; Engineer Reiji; with Medical Director Itsuki. The sequence ends with the silhouette of a spacewhale passing before a red supergiant.

Scene 1

The ship is seen in the mist of the Nebula, before cutting to Huro's face.

Huro: Spacewhale sighted! Battle stations. Launch the whaling pods.
Enid: This one's mine.

For the spacewhale, space was not an empty cold absence. It could feel the play of starlight on its skin, and the pull of gravity spread around it like an elastic sheet. It knew the neutrinos pouring through its body, its organs, even as, all around, quantum fluctuations flashed in and out of existence. It looped its tail and curved in wide swoops throughout the wide reaches of the cosmos.

The Hoshi-Henro launches its hunting ships and the great fight begins.

The whale had already passed and was threatening to outpace the crew so they set the engines to max and launched the hunting skiffs.

The Hoshi-Henro cut off the whale's escape with laser fire while the small ships chased, in order to get close enough to attack the beast with spacelances.

The whale turned, charging the first ship with its great head, splashing it to pieces with its sheer bulk. The crew, ejected in their spacesuit throw their lances at the whale but they bounce off harmlessly, finding no purchase. The other ships cluster around, and Huro springs his giant harpoon. It sinks into the belly of the whale which thrashes around, dragging Huro's ship after it, making it collide with another ship, breaking the harpoon's cord.

The Captain, standing tall, gets herself hoisted onto the spacewhale's back, brandishing her space lance. The whale tries to shake her off but she clings on. She is about to plunge the lance deep into the beast when she suddenly stands still and stiff, gradually floating into space off the whale's back.

Suddenly, just when victory seemed close, a great cry rang out from the whalers. 'The Captain, The Captain' they wailed. For the Captain has succumbed to a great infirmity. Though she lived and breathed, she was gone.

Flailing, the spacewhale departs and the whaling pods return to the main ship.

Scene 2

Enid's prone body is seen within sick bay. Huro and Dr Itsuki stand beside her.

Itsuki: She does not seem aware of where she is. It is almost as if she is in a coma. She does not respond to stimuli. It is serious.
Huro: But her eyes are still open and moving about.
Itsuki: But they never truly focus upon anything. It's as if she were not seeing what we were seeing.
Huro: Something happened to her in that nebula. Some effect upon her.
Itsuki: I haven't found anything in the blood samples. The disease is entirely mysterious.
Huro: we need to find out the cause of this new sickness.
Itsuki: That's why I've called for Eiko.

Eiko enters the medical cabin.

Eiko: Reporting for duty.
Itsuki: Eiko, I can care for them, I can test them. But we need to find out what is going on. We need to see what she is seeing. Only you can help us with that.

Enid's bed is wheeled into Eiko's lab.

Scene 3

Baleine, Pequod and Reiji are gathered in the atrium, with drinks. Through the large viewing windows they look out at the nebula which looks beautiful with splashed pinks and oranges.

Baleine: Almost like looking at the sunset, isn't it?
Pequod: I would hardly go that far. Impressive, but in its own way.
Reiji: I miss the earth. Sunsets. Real sunsets, seen through the atmosphere, breathing fresh air.

Baleine: How well do you remember them?
Reiji: I was eleven when the fleet took off, so I do remember them,
of course I do. But I hardly stared at them, you know. I didn't
realise they'd be so...I guess I took them for granted, didn't even
think that one day I would be missing them, and so didn't pay
attention.
Baleine: By that point in time, when we left, the pollution in the
atmosphere had reached such a point that every sunset and sunrise
diffused across the entire sky in a splash of colour. In a way it was
very striking, even if it was just achieved by the scattering of light
around the many dirt particles in the air. No, I remember those
earlier cool and compact sunrises, where you could see the disk of
the sun itself rising, if you were careful. But that was years before.
Pequod: You know what I never realised I'd miss? Rain. Rain on
my face.
Reiji: By the time we left it was so acidic that my mum ushered me
inside every time she saw a cloud.
Pequod: I even miss the sound of acid rain on my aluminium
umbrella.
Baleine: If we catch enough spacewhales we will have enough
Octavin to be able to make it to a new home planet. We'll get all
these things back.
Reiji: Enough spacewhales? After all these years we've never caught
one!
Pequod: Perhaps we should stop this, dreaming of earth, that was,
wishing away our lives for something that is gone, living in the
future for something that might be, one day?
Reiji: Yes.

They stare out again, looking at the vastness of space.

Baleine: Say something then.
Pequod: Have you heard anything about the Captain?
Baleine: It seemed like she sustained some sort of injury on the
hunt, what exactly it was, I have not been able to find out yet. She'll
pull through - it's Enid - she always does. She's strong.
Reiji: It sounded fairly bad. Not that I know the details.

Baleine: Huro and Itsuki are attending to her now.
Pequod: She was so close to landing the spacewhale. She was touching it, almost riding it.
Reiji: She'll be really annoyed with herself that she didn't manage to do it. Given how obsessed she is with the spacewhales.
Pequod: Good we ditched that inspector from the Octavin Corporation, or no doubt he would be lying into us now for our latest failure, restricting our rations again as a punishment.
Baleine: I think that we have not seen the last of Prebyn.
Pequod: Another drink?

Pequod gets some more drinks, and when he returns Reiji is waiting with an eager expression on her face and a pack of cards in her hands. She shuffles them expertly.

Reiji: Anyone want a game?
Pequod: Not your games again! Last time they didn't work, and you forgot the rules half way through.
Reiji: I've done some work on them since then.
Baleine: I for one am not interested.
Reiji: You're just scared that you're going to lose.
Baleine: I won't lose. I never lose games.
Reiji: What about that time when we did the spacecarp fishing contest?
Baleine: That was not a game, it was an activity vital for the functioning of the ship
Reiji: It was a contest though. And I did beat you on it.
Baleine: Fine. We'll do your game. But I'll only play if Pequod does.
Reiji: It needs three anyway.
Pequod: I don't get a choice?
Baleine: No.
Reiji: Game is simple. It's called Traitor. There are two identical packs of cards, and I am going to transfer one unknown card from the spare pack into the playing pack. With these 53 cards, we are each given five cards at the start, and the idea is to complete sets of number pairs by either taking a card each turn from the pile or

from another person. The loser is the person who gets left at the end with the extra card.

Pequod: So there isn't a winner…only a loser.

Reiji: The whole idea is to try and find out what the traitor card is and then try to avoid it.

Pequod: I'm not sure that the game will work.

Baleine: How about we make this more interesting? Let's do the strip version.

Reiji: Not again!

Pequod: Last time Huro put us in cabin arrest for a week.

Baleine: Then you shouldn't have lost.

Reiji: We'll play the regular way.

Pequod: If it even works.

Baleine: Set us up then Reiji.

Reiji starts to deal the cards out, and as she does so Pequod suddenly slumps back in her chair.

Reiji: I know you don't want to play but you can't just zone out in a sulk. You have to join in properly.

Baleine: Wait Reiji, I think something is wrong. He's not…Pequod? Pequod? Can you hear me?

Reiji: He's not responding.

Baleine: Get Dr Itsuki here right now!

Reiji: I'm not feeling great myself right now…I…I feel all faint, like I'm fading away…I…

Reiji slumps into her chair and her drink clatters to the floor, spilling everywhere.

Baleine: Something deeply wrong is happening. It's time to raise the alarm!

Baleine presses the alarm on her transponder just as she collapses with the others.

Scene 4

Itsuki: The disease is spreading...there isn't enough room for them
all.
Huro: we are converting the hanger bay into a temporary ward.
Itsuki: at this rate there will be none of us left
Huro: we need answers. We have no idea how the contagion is
spreading between crew members, except that it is passing quickly.
We are shutting down non essential operations and running the
ship on a skeleton crew.
Itsuki: the manner of infection is unclear, like everything else about
this disease. I've got my hands full caring for all these invalids. Eiko
is working as fast as she can to find out what is happening to us.
Huro: we should be able to manage until a cure is ready.
Itsuki: we may not have the luxury of time. Their vital signs are
fading. It's as if we are losing then. They're drifting away from us. If
this goes on too long…
Huro: Eiko needs to hurry up with her research.

Scene 5

Eiko in lab, setting up some equipment, when Huro enters

Huro: the disease is getting worse. We need answers now.
Eiko: there are many important questions. What is the nature of the
disease? What is its cause? How does it spread? Only after
answering these can a cure be attempted.
Huro: you must have made some progress?
Eiko: yes, look at this.

She shows him a device and screen that Enid is hooked up on.

Eiko: the eye movements plus lack of response pointed to some
sort of waking dream, so I hooked up into the neural processing

lobe of the brain. Look at the screen...this is what Enid is
experiencing.

Huro: it looks like...earth. and some sort of teaching facility. And
the Captain is one of the children? What is going on?
Eiko: in that world she is a school child.
Huro: can't we get her to look at us and the real world? Is she
aware at all?
Eiko: through my evaluations I can tell that she is aware of stimuli
here, but they appear in an altered form in her dream state. There
are points of contact with the real, true world, points where the
true world comes pouring through the torn fabric of space-time
and this illumines the rest. There is a sort of continuity between the
worlds, some sort of correspondence between them? Perhaps the
switching on of a light here is transformed into a sunrise there.
Maybe the sound of a swishing door here becomes the roll and roar
of a car there. Maybe the touch of hands on them here becomes
the brush of the wind there. Perhaps the voices of those who love
them only sound in the faint stirrings of their hearts. Shadows on
the wall.
Huro: So this disease causes her to believe that she is in a different
world, but we can still interact with her?
Eiko: Yes, but only tangentially. But the fascinating question is
why? Why is this symptom part of the pathology? Which brings me
to the brain scans.

She shows him a screen to one side.

Huro: what does this mean?
Eiko: if you look here, to the amygdala you can see there is a
speck...now take a look at this enlarged version?
Huro: what is that?

Eiko: it is an alien. Not a carbon based life form like us, it has a structure which means that it can easily pass through matter. Scanning the nebula we can see that it is infested.
Huro: then we better get out
Eiko: as soon as possible.

Huro picks up his transponder

Huro: order the immediate departure from the nebula
Bridge: the spacewhale is still out there!
Huro: do it. Take us far away.

Huro shuts it off

Eiko: it seems like the alien feeds off a particular type of brainwave frequency, and so induces this state within the person leading to this dream coma we have seen.
Huro: how do we get rid of them?
Eiko: based on their structure I have determined that they will be susceptible to radio waves. Based on a trial, they are.
Huro: well done. We will soon find a way to exit this disease. Blast them away!
Eiko: it is not so simple. When attacked by the radiation the alien tightens its grip on the brain and the toxins released into the blood increase in toxicity. Based on my extrapolations, if I were to directly attack the creature then it would result in the dream state becoming permanent, even if the alien were killed.
Huro: then what can we do?
Eiko: more tests. I suspect that we may have to examine the details of the dream state. If we cannot break it off from the outside we may be able to crack it open from the inside.

Scene 6
Noni, the keeper of the turtles, is sitting beside the fountain in the atrium at feeding time. Eiko approaches.

Noni: A pleasure to see you officer...I can't help but notice it is very quiet today.

Eiko: There is a terrible sickness spreading through the ship and we are defenceless against it. The disease is caused by aliens from the nebula.

Noni: Indeed.

Eiko: I would not otherwise ask, but everyone else is working flat out. Transmit this message to the fleet warning of this nebula. We cannot risk any other ships falling into this deadly hole.

Noni: But I had thought that the Hoshi-Henro was on bad terms with the remainder of the fleet? You recently ditched the Inspector which the Company sent to this ship, did you not?

Eiko: It is true that relations are...strained. But this is too important. We cannot gamble the survival of the human race on a petty squabble over quotas and yields.

Noni: I wonder if they will see it that way.

Eiko: It matters not. We have decided to send the message anyway.

Noni: I will arrange the transmission.

Scene 7

Production note: this scene contains the bulk of the exposition of the episode. In performance it should be spiced up to keep the interest of the casual viewer. Try cutting to some cute aliens to bounce around in jars as the explanation proceeds. At some point also, as a visual representation, get a piece of paper, turn it on itself and poke a pencil through, to indicate moving from one world to another. It is obligatory in scenes of this type - a ruling from the Writers Guild.

In her lab, Eiko is busy connecting wires when Itsuki arrives.

Itsuki: I linked up all the patients to your rig like you asked. What do you find?

Eiko: something incredible, even more than I thought I would find. I found by cross reference that the dream state is shared...the aliens have a psychic link to each other, and the hosts become connected...

Itsuki: what does that mean?

Eiko: there is a whole alternative society submerged below the surface of the mind.

Itsuki: Have you managed to progress with some hope of a cure?

Eiko: the key thing is to starve the aliens from the brainwaves...then they will disengage and leave.

Itsuki: but your report said we can't blast them with radiation to make them disengage.

Eiko: yes, we will have to try to induce the person to wake up and overcome the signals from the aliens. We need to wake them up from the inside.

Itsuki: but we can only do that if we get inside the dream state and communicate with them

Eiko: correct. So I have been working on how to communicate with this other world. It seems from my investigations that their world dream is based on earth as it was. A dream of history, a safe and controlled world with trees and wind and rain.

Itsuki: it is hardly surprising, faced with the immensity of space that the human mind seeks refuge in an idealised past. A fantasy.

Eiko: the most difficult thing is that their dream minds reject any sense of the real world as implausible and unlikely.

Itsuki: they barely notice our voices, how can you communicate into their world, even talk to them about the things that now seemingly are important to them?

Eiko: I have found a way to introduce a modification into their dream world. Something not so unusual so that it is not rejected outright by the sleeping mind. The aim is to create a sort of meeting place, a neutral place, in order to converse through Virtual Reality. Drawing on some historical records I have therefore made a city to serve as the ground for this...I have called it Dunwich.

Itsuki: is it ready to put into action?

Eiko: almost we will be able to and then hear their own minds...the most difficult thing was within this construct to introduce our world in an innocuous way

Itsuki: what have you done?

Eiko: I am afraid that I have turned us into a mere TV show within their world. They watch the Hoshi-Henro show.

Itsuki: well I never!
Eiko: It will be a difficult process, to get them to believe that the
TV show is in fact the reality and then get them to wake themselves
Itsuki: can't you introduce something in their own world, some sort
of magical item which they can use to wake themselves? That
seems to be the way to do it, to perform the extraction from within.
Eiko: Let's go for technology not magic: A Reality Alteration
Device.
Itsuki: Or you could start the rumour that there are certain places
where the boundaries between the worlds are thin and they can
step through - portal.
Eiko: It will work. But the hardest stage of all will be getting them
to believe.
Itsuki: The faster we can talk with them the better.

Scene 8

In her lab Eiko is preparing Huro for the next phase of testing on Enid.

Eiko: The trial is ready. Plug yourself in. You will see what she sees
but you will not be a person in that dream world. You will be
something akin to a voice in her head - and I will stimulate her
anterior cortex so that she responds by speaking out loud.
Huro: strap me in.
Eiko: Yes commander. I think you will find her mind is quite
receptive.

Eiko straps him in.

Huro: Enid, come back to us.
Enid: Wha? Where?
Huro: I am standing on a spaceship, the Hoshi-Henro. I am Huro.
We have stood together many times, fought side by side, faced
down fierce foes.
Enid: Huro, you say?
Huro: Enid, listen now, this is important. The Hoshi-Henro is your
real home. You are our Captain, here with us. The world all around

you is not the real world. Be not deceived. You belong here with us, not lost in sleep. You must come to us here. You must return.
Enid: Yes...yes...I can see it now. I believe...I am the Captain of the Hoshi-Henro, I am not defined by what seems to be the case here.
Huro: Listen to me Enid. You must find the Reality Alteration Device, so that you can return to us here and leave the world of your dream.
Enid: If that is the way to gain my restoration, that is what I will do.
Huro: We have managed to insert it within the dream world. You must find it. Do you know where it is?
Enid: It is...it is coming. They are bringing it to London, to the exhibition. I will go and get it there.
Huro: Yes, proceed.
Enid: I have the tickets, I have made the arrangements...the time is drawing close now.
Huro: Yes, stretch out and reach for it.
Enid: The RAD is near. I am so close to gaining it, to returning to the stars.
Huro: You must lay your hands upon it.
Enid: No, they're stopping me. They won't let me on the train.
Huro: Fight to get back.
Enid: They've got me, they've...
Itsuki: She's struggling.
Enid: I have lost my chance. The RAD has gone.
She gasps.
Enid: All is gone. All hope is lost.
Huro: No. Don't talk like that Captain Toxequo. Hope is never gone. There always remains - Captain - Enid!

Enid slumps into a deeper sleep

Eiko: The attempt has exhausted her. She will need time to recover.
Huro: Can you arrange a different extraction, this one I doubt will work
Itsuki: we have no other plan.

Enid remains in the coma. Their attempt to rescue her has failed.

Scene 9

Eiko enters the Ship's Control Room. All the lights are flashing and there is only one person managing all the consoles, rushing from one to the other.

Eiko: what is happening here?
Person: I am the entirety of the bridge staff today.

There is a deep groan beneath them and a terrible shudder goes through the ship.

Eiko: What was that?
Person: I'll find out.

She goes to one of the nearby computer screens.

Person: There's been a hull breach. There aren't enough of us to care for the ship, and there is no leadership. We're sinking here.
Eiko: It shouldn't be just you here. And there should be a member of the command staff here. Why are there no officers?
Person: no orders have been sent out.
Eiko: what? Huro in the Captain's absence should be here. Where is he, what is he doing?
Person: I heard he was in the medical cabin. He won't leave or deal with any other business.
Eiko: We will see about that.

Scene 10

In sick bay where Enid has been returned for a transfusion. Huro is sitting beside the Captain's bed. Itsuki greets Eiko.

Eiko: what are my orders?
Itsuki: you have received them already. Keep on working on a cure.

Eiko: Huro should not be sitting there. He should be commanding the ship.

Itsuki: It is no good to save the ship but lose our Captain.

Eiko: yes but he's not saving her. He's holding her hand and she isn't even conscious. It is a waste.

Itsuki: He's trying to wake her, to lead her back to this world.

Eiko: Is that even scientifically possible?

Itsuki: For those as close as our Captain and Huro...all they've been through over the years...the neural pathways associated with each other will be stronger and more habitable than anything else...the bond they have as partners working together in a great enterprise, there are few things stronger...maybe he can bring her back, if anyone can...maybe he can get her mind to fight whatever it is in there, whatever is eating away at her.

Eiko: It sounds like a long shot to me, a baseless hope. There is no evidence it will work.

Itsuki: But Huro must try. How could he live with himself if she is lost and he did not do everything in his power to assist her.

Eiko: I question how appropriate it is for an auxiliary to show such devotion to his commanding officer. It suggests that his attachment might be more than professional; that there might be a romantic element. And we all know that it would be forbidden under the Company Code.

Itsuki: You don't have problems breaking the company code when it suits you.

Eiko: That was different.

Itsuki: Here's what I think is going on. You're looking at the Captain and Huro and you're wondering whether anyone would do that for you. And you're not sure and you don't know how to feel or what to say because you're afraid that you'll always be alone, and never connect, really connect, with another human.

Eiko: I don't see how any of that is relevant to subsection 5c of the Company Code or our current need for executive leadership.

Itsuki: You want your orders. Here's some from me. Grow a heart. And don't you dare answer by talking about the cardiac organ.

Eiko: I will endeavour to follow my orders.

Scene 11

Itsuki stands above Reiji's bed, hesitating over whether to touch her.
Itsuki: Reiji, I know you can't hear me. I hope that you're ok in there….we haven't...we didn't leave things in a good place between us. That was mostly my fault, and...I want to say I'm sorry. It's a little cowardly to speak to you when you can't answer back, when you probably can't even register it at all. But I need to tell you in some form...

Itsuki wipes her forehead which had become beaded with perspiration.
Itsuki: I know you've moved on now from what we had together, and it's a good thing. But I haven't managed to get that far yet. I've got stuck. There was so much left unsaid that I needed to tell you. For my sake not for yours...I guess I'll take this as my opportunity.

He sits down beside her to tell her more.

Scene 12

A shot of the human fleet before going to a close up of the HQ ship for The Octavin Corporation.

Staff member: We have received a transmission from
Commissioner: They dare to contact us after what they have done? No matter. It seems they want us to stay away from these coordinates. Contact Prebyn and order him to investigate in his new ship, and to bring us back news of what he has found.
Staff member: But what if the sickness is real?
Commissioner: Then it will offer us the perfect opportunity to capture the weakened ship.

Scene 13

An alarm sounds, Itsuki, Huro, Eiko, gather around Enid's bed.

Itsuki: There isn't much time left. Her vital functions are growing weaker.
Eiko: We have to connect with her, this is our last chance!

Huro: I will speak to her, I will guide her back.
Eiko: But-
Huro: Do it!

Eiko hooks up Huro.

Huro: Enid, it's me, Huro. I'm here. I'm going to guide you back
home.
Eiko: What is she doing now?
Huro: What are you doing Enid? Captain?
Enid: I'm looking for a way back. But it's so hard.
Huro: She is searching for a portal, an opening in the dream world,
to return her to here.
Enid: Maybe on the next mountain...the next valley. I won't stop
until I reach it.
Itsuki: Her pulse is barely there. The dream world is threatening to
swallow her up, and take her life with it. She's getting weaker by the
second.
Enid: Up the hill in the crease of the rock strewn path, a breeze
blowing down, smelling of something long forgotten.
Huro: Come on Enid.
Enid: the portal has shifted!
Huro: Enid, if ever we needed you, now is the time.
He grasps her hand.
Enid: Cetasta!

*In her dream state Captain Enid hears the voice of someone she loves. At first
it sounds distant and threatening. But gradually as she awakes it becomes
clearer and sweeter. Her eyes blink open and she awakes fully. She breathes a
long sigh, and raises herself.*

Enid: I've had the strangest dream!
Huro: Captain!
Itsuki: You're back.
Enid: I thought I was...

Eiko: You had been infected in the brain by an alien creature that took over your functioning. It will be coming loose now. Wait, I will irradiate it.

Eiko works a complicated looking machine.

Eiko: It is gone now.
Huro: We are in a struggle. Most of the crew have succumbed. The ship is falling apart. We are on the verge of...drifting loose through space.
Enid: What has happened to my ship?
Itsuki: It lacked a Captain.
Enid: I feel my strength returning to me. Stand by for action!
Eiko: Captain! You really are back!
Enid: Let us press forward: let's get this turtle swimming!
Itsuki: Yes Captain.
Enid: We will press on and rescue our crew from this invasion. We will pull Barry out from that maw.
Itsuki: Barry?
Enid: I mean Pequod. And all the others too. We will not allow them to be lost. We will pull them out into reality.

Scene 14

Eiko and Enid in the lab with Reiji prone lying down in the dream state...

Eiko: Let me explain how I-
Enid: No need. I will call them as their Captain.
Eiko: But-
Enid: Don't forget. I have been in there. I know what it's like. I know how to guide them back.
Eiko: But-
Enid: Set it up. We will try Reiji first. She has an innate understanding of machinery. She will be able to construct something according to my directions.
Eiko: Wouldn't she have forgotten herself, and all her skills?

Enid: Even if she has, she will still feel the loss of it. And that will be enough.

Enid: Reiji, what do you call yourself there?
Reiji: Izzy.
Enid: Izzy, I know that you can only hear a faint echo of what I am saying. But that is still of some use. I am going to guide you to build a Reality Alteration Device.
Reiji: What is that?
Enid: It is a technology that will form a path to the stars, to the world of Hoshi-Henro and spacewhales. It will bring you home.
Reiji: But Hoshi-Henro is only a TV show.
Enid: No, it is real. The most real thing in the world. It's your dream world that only contains fragments of reality. Together we will push through the fogs of ignorance…
Reiji: Everyone will think I'm crazy.
Enid: Then don't tell everyone. Or at least, only those who you can see in their eyes that they too know that the world is more than it seems.
Reiji: I am ready to start work.
Enid: What you need to do is to collapse the subsidiary frame into the main frame of reference. This is best done through a precisely calculated explosion which uses antimatter to negate the surroundings, whilst protecting you with a strong electromagnetic field. You must then step within this portal that is created.
Reiji: I am working on it. I am gathering the materials I have done the calculations and the equations. I believe it should work.
Enid: Try it!
Reiji: It isn't working….
Enid: Try again. It might have needed a test run.
Reiji: I've tried now…tried many times over. But it won't work. It can't work. I'm struggling. I'm a wreck now…I…
Enid: You need to-

Reiji: It isn't working. It just...I can't do it. And most likely the reason I can't do it is that there is no other world and I am going crazy right now. I need to stop trying, to become sane again.
Enid: No, you are almost there. Only the most difficult stage remains. Time in the dream world works differently from time here in the real world. It becomes at times compressed, at other times elongated, and mixed up all around. Your device needs to take note of this. You need not to treat time as a linear constant but in a sort of spiral spring that itself can move. You need to model for that.
Reiji: I'll input that, but I don't expect it to...it's working! The test experiment worked! I'll tell Dr Hincliffe and then I'll use it. I'll come and step through into the stars. I'll-

Reiji opens her eyes.
Enid: Reiji! You came out!
Reiji: Captain! I can't- I- It's- It's just so overwhelming-
Enid: You really are here, in the Hoshi-Henro. You can relax now.
Reiji: But how...how did this happen?
Enid: We are being attacked by a space sickness caused by aliens rooting in our brains. But we have found a way to fight it. The both of us are proof of that.
Reiji: Then let me join the fight!

Scene 15
In the Control Room, Eiko approaches Enid.

Eiko: captain I have found a way to communicate with the aliens. Perhaps we're on the wrong track. It could be that they don't mean harm...we must talk to them...
Enid: It is worth a try. I'll let you take the lead on this one. Put it on the screen.

Eiko presses a button and twists a dial and a creepy green octopussy creature appears on the screen.

Eiko: We come in peace. You might not realise this but in your desire to feed you are destroying our ship! You have spread a disease around the crew. Please disengage.
Alien: There is no disease. Only salvation.
Eiko: No it is definitely a disease.
Alien: No your true home is earth. We are taking you all back. You have been looking for your home for many years. This is your path back. You can stop searching now.
Eiko: But it's a lie! This disease is a terrible deception.
Alien: No, it is you who have been deceived. It is your lives that...don't you see? None of this is real. We aren't in space at all but dreaming on earth. We are actors who have got caught up in our roles and have forgotten that this is only an entertainment programme. A TV show. We need to break loose from this fantasy and return to the real world. We are stuck and trapped here. I am returning you to the world of green growing grass and waves crashing on the sand and the cycling seasons. Home. For the coarse touch of reality on our fingers. I will save you all from this dream world...an epidemic will be unleashed. You can enjoy your life on the once-vanished earth again. You're welcome.
Eiko: But that is simply absurd. We are not figments of the imagination, but real actual people.
Alien: It shows the depth of the deception, doesn't it. Don't you want to enjoy the gentle sunlight again. Don't you wish to enjoy all the goodness of the earth. Don't deny it any longer. Come back to it, stop trying continually to escape.
Eiko: We are not the ones trying to escape. Who would escape here, with the troubles that continually assault us, the privations we must suffer, the barrenness of space?
Alien: Come now, it is a world with a happy ending.
Eiko: What's wrong with a happy ending?
Alien: Happy endings aren't true. They are fairy tales. Everyone knows that the real world is the one which is shot through with unbearable sadness, which only has to offer death. Which is all about getting all you can before you slide into oblivion.
Eiko: But-

Enid: Enough. I have heard it all before, sunk down in the depths
of the dream-world. That all there is to the world is that which can
be sensed and recorded and quantified and sold and won. That
beauty is an irrelevance and truth impossible and goodness
subjective. But whatever else I do not know, and I am sure there is
a lot, I am sure that the universe does exist, that a true reality is
possible.
Alien: Have you not considered, that even now your reality might
not be ultimate, there might be an even greater wakefulness to
which you might rise?
Enid: It is possible. Our journey here is not over. Although our
eyes have been unveiled we are still pilgrims through the stars. We
have yet to find our final resting place, our ultimate home.
Alien: I can see that your dogmatic rigidness when it comes to
these beliefs cannot be-
Enid: I've had enough. Eiko, blast it.
Eiko: Yes Captain.

*The alien is destroyed. Try and get some exploding green goo to show this
visually.*

Scene 16

Pequod is lying before Enid and Eiko in the medical cabin.

Eiko: It's all ready. You can begin now, the rescue of Pequod.
Enid: It won't be the same as Izzy. I mean Reiji. Barry is a different
type of fish.

They draw close to Pequod.

Enid: Barry, can you hear me. It's Enid?
Pequod: Enid...Enid vanished a long time ago. Lost in the
mountains.
Enid: Can you tell me about the Reality Alteration Device. Are you
still working on it?

Pequod: Yes, I'm trying. Trying as hard as I can. I'm putting in the hours

Enid: Keep on going.

Pequod: Why do I feel so lost. I want to lie down and be quiet and for everyone to leave me alone. To have some time without them poking at me, trying to get something out of me.

Enid: You feel like that because you don't belong there, in that world. Now is not the time to give up, not when you're so close to leaving that situation. Just a bit longer.

Pequod: I can't get it to work. The RAD. It won't...I'm such a loser...I'm not able to do anything.

Enid: What have you done so far?

Pequod: I am able to get the two frames of reference clear, and according to my calculations they should be collapsing into each other but it isn't working.

Enid: You need to twist the frame of reference to correct for the time dilation.

Pequod: It isn't working.

Enid: You need to-

Pequod: Arrrgggghh. I can't...it isn't working because it's all a lie. Because it isn't true and I'm just trying to kid myself. There is no world of Hoshi-Henro. It's only a TV show. And Enid didn't vanish. She died/

Enid: No.

Pequod: Can I bear to admit it? I'd rather die.

Enid: Continue with the RAD, just one more evaluation and you'll crack it.

Pequod: What am I saying? I'll decline. I'll accept this world. I'll come to terms with it and grow up. It wasn't what I hoped it could be. The universe is a dreary place, I had better get used to it.

Enid: Please Pequod.

There are some disquieting beeps and Pequod grows quiet.

Eiko: He has disengaged from the simulation program.

Enid: We lost him.

Eiko: Try again, he will be re-established soon.

Enid: I don't think the plan to introduce the RAD concept will work with Barry. I will have to come at it from a different direction.

Eiko presses some buttons and Pequod can be seen moving.

Eiko: You can try again now, he has re-engaged.
Enid: Barry, this is Enid here. I know that you can't hear me properly, or only a distorted echo, or something. I wonder what it felt when you first saw me in that dream world. Some twinge of recognition? Some strange resonance. A cry of unmet distorted desire? All you knew, I'd bet, was some sort of unfulfilled longing that called you further on. And then, I remember, we got to know each other in that dream world. You were never as confident of your true identity, but I led you on to discover it, through adventures and betrayal and hope. Our paths separated in that dream world, but still we wrote and I urged you to continue the quest to return to our true home in the stars. But then I left - was I too early, should I have stayed longer to bring you with me? - and you had to manage by yourself. And you couldn't sustain the faith and you gave up. Until much later you knew that someone else had been plucked out of the dream world, blinking into the sunlight. Then something in you reawakened and you realised that this wasn't an obscure hobby but the essence of life itself. You realised that I returned to the stars, and your student Izzy. That it is absolutely, undeniably true. There is nothing now preventing you from following. Can you tread where we have gone before? Can you put your feet in our footmarks, where we have trod out the way before you and broken the barrier between the worlds. Yes, you can do it. We have made the way. You must only follow.
Pequod: But there is a weight on me, a great weight that bows me down. I cannot even move.
Enid: It is nothing to me...out in the marshes I am creating a portal, just like the one I entered through. You must go there and fling yourself through.
Pequod: It is foggy out there…
Enid: enter through the mists, the portal is there.

Pequod: I've left the house, I'm walking along. I'm going down the footpaths and out into the channels and pools. I can barely see in front of me...except, over there, a patch of fog which seems to have a different texture, a different movement...wait...it must be the portal.

He hesitated, there on the brink...
Pequod: I can't do it. I just can't.
Enid: Breathe.
Pequod: I feel something. A breeze flowing through. And the fragrance...I can't quite say what it is. But it reminds me...it reminds me of something I've lost but I can't say what it is.
Enid: Rest.
Pequod: Yes.

Pequod enters through the portal, and his eyes open.

Pequod: Enid?
Enid: Barry! Or should I say Pequod!
Eiko: Congratulations, you made it.
Pequod: But am I really here?
Enid: Yes, this is the Hoshi-Henro where I am the Captain, where we travel through the stars.
Pequod: I can't believe it! It's like I'm dreaming and any moment will have to come back down to reality.
Enid: No, this is the reality. That dream world is passing away. It has no future. This is the place where everything real is to be found. This is the place where there is life and living.
Pequod: Yes. But above all Enid, I'm so glad that I've found you again. To live in that place without you...I was going through hell...but now I've found you...only it was you who found me, you who rescued me...I'm so happy to be back.
Enid: Welcome home.

Scene 17

Enid: You won't believe how real it felt.
Itsuki: I can't believe you thought it was real.
Enid: It was real in its own way, but at the same time I knew it was missing something I couldn't name. Like I was homesick for a home that I could not remember. Like I was longing for something but I could never say what it was.
Huro: You're back now.
Itsuki: There still is much need out there. Many are afflicted.

They all look grave for a moment.

Eiko: Baleine is still under.
Pequod: Amy!
Reiji: Mum?! No wonder. That's a little bit sick.
Itsuki: Blame your own subconscious.
Eiko: We must bring her out too.
Huro: What about the rest of the crew? They must be saved also.
Enid: It is not just our crew. It is the whole fleet. I received this communication just now:

SOS - the fleet has become infected with a space sickness which leaves those who succumb insensible to the world. The disease has spread, and the vast majority of us are now immobile and unresponsive. There are few of us left. Cure procurement now essential for the survival of the human race. End.

Pequod: But how did the fleet get infected?
Eiko: The aliens must have piggybacked the signal we sent.
Reiji: How is that even possible?
Pequod: It could have been a more nefarious infection route.
Enid: I don't know how it happened, but it's happened and it means our problem got a whole lot bigger. Now the entirety of humanity is becoming infected and entering the dream state, being lost to the world.
Itsuki: we will have to act to rescue them

Huro: No problem. We have proved we can extract people. The Captain and Reiji and Pequod.

Eiko: But it took too long. If we give that much time to each person...they won't last, the disease will overcome them. Not if the entire fleet is infected.

Itsuki: Eiko is right. We cannot save one by one like this...we will never be able to do it like that. We will have to develop another way.

Pequod: But we have found no other way.

Enid: No (*softly*)

Itsuki: What?

Enid: There is another way.

Eiko: How then?

Enid: One of us will have to enter fully into the world of their dream. To fully go in, not communicate at a distance through virtual reality, to become just like the others. That person would take the infection voluntarily upon themself and then break open the entire system from within. That person would show them the truth of reality. That person will have to wrench them all back to having the right relationship to reality. That person would have to bring the weight of reality into their ignorance and shatter it so it was no more. Light into darkness.

Pequod: But who would have the self-possession to enter without being deceived themselves? Who could, who would, voluntarily bear the weight for that infection for others? Who of us has the strength, the will, the sheer love to enter into the world of shadows for their sake?

Huro: Who indeed?

To Be Continued...

AFTERWORD

Thank you for agreeing to take part in the Reality Adjustment Programme and for reading the preparatory documentation. You are now ready to receive treatment: please move from the waiting room to the Adjustment Room, where Dr Eiko will assist you.

It may not seem to you that you are currently in a waiting room. It might seem to you as an armchair at home, a train, a coffee shop, the beach, your bed. The doorway you can see may well seem to be an ordinary door frame that you have walked through many times before.

But by now your mind may have been opened to such an extent that you are able to conceive the possibility that the world is not as it seems. We assure you that there are deeper currents and stronger tides than those accessible by sense perception. We invite you to open yourself further and enter into the greater reality. All it takes is a few steps. Dr Eiko is waiting.

Acknowledgements

Enid's diary is based on Don Quixote, and her name, Enid Toxequo, is an anagram of his. The Hoshi-Henro show is largely Moby Dick in space. A week in the life of Amy Wu is based upon Pride & Prejudice. Plato's analogy of the cave provides the metaphysics throughout.